THE BICYCLE EATER

Larry Tremblay

Translated by Sheila Fischman

Talonbooks
Vancouver

Talonbooks
P.O. Box 2076, Vancouver, British Columbia, Canada V6B 3S3
www.talonbooks.com

Typeset in Sabon and printed and bound in Canada.

First Printing: 2005

BRITISH COLUMBIA ARTS COUNCIL
Supported by the Province of British Columbia

Canada Council for the Arts   Conseil des Arts du Canada

Canada

The publisher gratefully acknowledges the financial support of the Canada Council for the Arts; the Government of Canada through the Book Publishing Industry Development Program; and the Province of British Columbia through the British Columbia Arts Council for our publishing activities.

First published in French in 2002 as *Le Mangeur de bicyclette* by Les Editions Leméac, Montreal.

LIBRARY AND ARCHIVES CANADA CATALOGUING IN PUBLICATION

Tremblay, Larry, 1954–
[Mangeur de bicyclette. English]
    The bicycle eater / Larry Tremblay ; translated by Sheila Fischman.

Translation of: Le mangeur de bicyclette.
ISBN 0-88922-528-1

    I. Fischman, Sheila II. Title. III. Title: Mangeur de bicyclette. English.

PS8589.R445M3613 2005   C843'.54   C2005-902470-4

for Rolf

PART ONE: A FOUR-LETTER GHOST

☙

PART TWO: THE NIGHT OF THE BUTTERFLIES

☙

PART THREE: BEAUTY FALLEN FROM THE SKY

☙

Part One

A FOUR-LETTER GHOST

1

While Drinking a *Mort Subite*

A GIRL, that's right, a girl, had just taken a seat at my table. It wasn't Anna, but it was a girl. Had she confused me with someone else? Now that she was seated, it was hard for her to back-pedal. And yet, no. She really had come towards me and she knew perfectly well what she was doing. The way she'd done it was a clear sign of her decisiveness.

What a discovery! That girl had sat at my table because she'd wanted to and still did. An inner tightness was creeping over me. It was transformed into pure emotion when I looked up at the clock that gleamed above the bar: precisely 10:00 P.M. That girl had seated herself at my table at exactly the time of my date with Anna.

That girl couldn't be some ordinary girl setting out in my direction on a carefree Saturday night that didn't give a damn about whatever dates it made happen. No. This girl was THE girl. She'd sat down on the stroke of 10:00 P.M. She wasn't Anna. She was the only door I could open at that moment in my life. I had every reason to be impressed by the gaze that she levelled at me in spite of the dark glasses she was wearing in the middle of the night, which, it seemed to me, had draped her from head to toe in a second night, a prelude to thrilling flashes of inspiration.

I heard your mocking laughter, Anna. That this phoney mystery girl should deign to grant me a minimum of her attention was enough for me to give your ghost a flick and send it packing.

Ah, that four-letter ghost! I took it with me everywhere. In the end, its company had reduced me to a nervous tic: speaking the name of Anna till the letters were worn out. And what letters: a big *A*, twin *n*s, and a second *a* that was a smaller repetition of the first!

I had become the man who spoke the name of Anna. My situation was getting worse. The name was gaining ground, eating up other words or combining with them. I had even put down on paper an *annalexicon*. I'd left excerpts of it on Anna's voice mail. I hoped that would persuade her to respond to my invitations. At the Slow-Boeing that evening, while drinking a raspberry *Mort Subite*, I waited for her to appear. It was my seventh date. Anna hadn't shown up for the previous six. To make the waiting easier I talked to the four-letter ghost: "To say you, Anna, to tell you, ah! To recount you, Anna parade who moves through my life without even looking at me, ah! To say you, Anna wave, to tell you, to recount you, Anna parachute-blues, ah! To recount you, Anna catastrophe, Anna bubble that bursts in the faces of passers-by and spirits, to recount you, Anna embargo, Anna iceberg, to recount you ... "

I'd had to break off my prayer to Anna. THE girl had sat down at my table.

My hope of seeing Anna appear one Saturday night collapsed in one fell swoop. Translation: I'd just made up my mind to love THE girl, with no fuss, no muss, no haggling. To love her. To love her immediately, without wasting a second. To love her because not to love her would have meant a kind of suffering that dismembered me and scattered me into the roaring night. To love her because my body was liable to suffer the fate of merchandise past its prime. To love her without asking a single question because to question love makes it deteriorate. To love, then, the row of little teeth that two lips of an outmoded mauve colour had just revealed in a sketch of a smile. Because the girl, who definitely was not Anna, was quietly smiling at me.

How to approach her? How to find the front door? And most of all, where to ring the bell that would make her open the door and let me in? So far, I'd done nothing except turn to stone before the lightness of her long-lasting smile. The slightest error on my part would send me back to square one and I would languish with Anna's ghost till dawn. I went back to the verb *to love* and slipped it onto the girl's body as discreetly as I could—the better to record in detail the happiness that was falling onto me. She had a weird hairdo. No girl nowadays would dare to appear in public with her hair like Ginger's on *Gilligan's Island*. Only her. I concluded that her courage was equal to anything. Fortunately, she was shorter than Ginger, which reassured me. I'm attracted to bodies that match my own measurements.

Again I checked the time on the clock. Two minutes had passed since she'd appeared. So far so good. Neither of us had moved a muscle. I started to hail a passing waiter, then stopped. No, no, don't be hasty. A normal man would have already offered her a drink, something hard, maybe, as we put it so elegantly. Not me. I would never fall into that trap. I'd have to analyze the situation properly. She had taken a seat at my table. She hadn't opened her mouth to preface her act with a polite word or two, something to establish a kind of contract between the parties. Between us there was, so far, nothing. And that *nothing* was a valuable asset. A granite meteor sparkling in this bar made of chrome, glass, and plywood, materials very fashionable in Montreal at the time. Why scrape that *nothing*? Let's wait. Yes, wait! Hadn't I already waited too long? Didn't *waiting* sum up my personal tragedy? It did. And so what? Why beat around the bush? Was that girl, that woman, challenging me to make the first move, to speak to her? How was I supposed to know?

I felt faint. I'd just realized that, engrossed in my own thoughts as I was, I had no idea what expression I was showing her. A smile to match her own? I couldn't remember. One thing is certain, it wasn't what I was doing when she turned slightly and gave me the chance to fall in love with her profile too. I had to make a move. Wasn't she about to eject herself from her seat, offended by my attitude? I took the plunge. Opened my mouth. Heard myself offer her a *Mort Subite*—sudden death. Nothing. I repeated the offer. Nothing. She hadn't felt the slightest thrill. Totally insensitive to my offer, to my voice, my presence, my love, my ruin. I held out my arm and touched her. She started. She opened her purse, took out pad and pencil. Quickly scribbled something and gave it to me to read.

"I'm a deaf-mute. I think you're provocative."

Which brought tears to my eyes. I tried to hold them back, send them back to their source. How would she have interpreted such a liquid? I opened my mouth and exclaimed: "A deaf-mute, eh? It really doesn't show!" I realized how idiotic that was. Smiling, she handed me the pencil. It was my turn to write in the little notepad. I thought I'd start by saying, "My name is Christophe, I'm twenty-eight years old, I'm a photographer," but then I thought better of it, inclining instead towards a question along the lines of, "Do you like raspberry *Mort Subite*?" I rejected that very quickly though, in favour of something more personal and, in particular, more engaging. She had written that she thought I was provocative. I had to show that I felt equal to it. I'd have to write something that would express my love for her at the outset (it would have been simplest just to write the very classic and always effective "I love you"), but I was afraid the word *love* or its derivatives would scare her off. Too late is pointless, too soon is inconvenient. But was I sure that I loved her? Do you have to know someone before you can declare that you're in love? What do you know about someone when you love? If I love, I don't know. If I don't love, I have all the time in the world to get to know the person. Definitely, the first words spoken to someone when set down on paper are crucially important. Finally, I wrote: "What do you think of this bar?" A question to which she replied: "It's wonderful because it has you in it." I was flabbergasted. The tears I was holding back sank into the void of this Saturday night.

Michèle—that was her name—displayed an undeniable attraction towards my person. I was shaken. Strangled with joy. Also by fear. Especially by fear, because my Mexican incidents made me anticipate the worst whenever a little light was flickering at the end of the tunnel of my bad luck. But I'd decided that this Saturday evening would be memorable, an evening blessed among all. Anna that's all, I dismissed your ghost forever and ever, amen. Told it to go to hell. Michèle had accepted my invitation to end the evening at my place.

As soon as I saw her stand up when we were about to leave the Slow-Boeing, I was disappointed. I had seen, known, loved Michèle only when she was sitting across from me. I hadn't even imagined her any other way. Once she was on her feet, I considered her to be too small. I also thought that it was petty of me to pass such judgement on someone I had decided to love utterly. She wasn't too small. I was the one who lacked grandeur. For over an hour, we had been a seated couple, happy and carefree, exchanging light-hearted banter on a notepad. Now it was time to move on to another stage, not look for excuses to postpone the normal course of events. Michèle's proportions were perfect. Her height and her gait made you want to protect her, envelop her, defend her. No, what stood out was her leather jacket; it was too heavy, too bulky, seemed to belong to another time or another story. I wasn't fooled though. Anna and I were exactly the same height. I would have to get used to straying from the beaten path. I must stop using Anna as a universal measurement. In any case, as we were crossing Saint-Louis Square to get to my place on Coloniale Avenue, I'd put my arm around Michèle's shoulders and an exquisite sensation convinced me that I was the happiest man on earth.

Opening the door to my apartment, I felt the first shivers of fever. An attack was on the way. Since my return from Mexico, I'd been floating in a world of dreams, hallucinations, and memories. All because of a Caribbean jellyfish that had burned my leg and injected me with a poison unknown to all the doctors I'd consulted. That evening, I absolutely must not fall back into those troubled waters. I shut the door behind me, anxious.

With a profusion of gestures and facial expressions, Michèle went into ecstasy over my apartment, which I personally had long ago declared to be a disaster area. In summer, the walls oozed. In winter, the paint peeled, falling like dandruff into the dry air overheated by radiators that I couldn't control. The fragmented style of my interior decoration was due to the explosive nature of my artistic production. I was a photographer. And I persisted. There was an exhibition of my works in the apartment, permanent and in free fall, works that were self-destructing under dust and anonymity. They littered the floor, they papered the walls. Like so many artists in town, I'd gone through a "staircases and fire hydrants" phase, photographing them from every angle, in every season, in the rain, the snow, at dawn, at dusk. Which meant there was a lot of grey. I preferred my more rosy "Anna" phase, even if, over time, she looked more red to me. Michèle looked greedily, eyes wide, mouth opening in oohs and ahs. My artist's vanity left her free to exclaim. I took my leave of her and went into the bathroom.

A quick look in the mirror above the sink confirmed that I was well and truly about to enter a transformative phase: sweat on my forehead, gaze lost in a mist that heralded a storm. I gulped four aspirins, splashed my face with cold water, then went back to join Michèle who was looking at one of my three-dimensional pieces—the only one, actually. She held out her notepad. "It looks like a coat." Taking her pen to write a response I brushed her hand. Driven by an instinct I couldn't control, I grabbed it and brought it to my lips. The fragrance of her skin went to my head. I made every effort to think of something to put down about my first and certainly my last three-dimensional work. "It used to be a coat. Now it's a sculpture. I mean, I hope it is. Dig around in the left pocket. There's a short text that completes the meaning of the piece." Like a well-brought-up child, Michèle did as she was told. She found the text and glanced at it, a smile in her eyes.

RECONSTRUCTION OF A THING THAT NEVER HAPPENED

One evening I followed a girl who was wearing the same coat that you had at the time, when I dreamed

*that we were dancing, clad only in our sweat. The
girl, I had cornered at the end of a lane near Duluth
Street. Tearing off her coat didn't leave a puddle on
the pavement, already broken up by an early winter.
Vinyl coat, 2:00 A.M., no moon, no hope, not a soul.
Black coat, flaking sleeves, pink lining. I cooked it. I
boiled it. I flung it outside, onto my gallery, between
two chairs. It laughed, it cracked. It became
impossible to ignore: a heap of love. I turned it into
a neurotic work of art. I exhibited it in my living
room under the theme "Reconstruction of a Thing
That Never Happened." It stinks. I tolerate it. And
that's that. Now what? I make myself coffee and I
avoid drawing you inside my closed eyes. I'm afraid
that my eye-teeth will cross my mind and bite. I
loathe Prince Arthur Street, disappearing under the
crowds of suburban tourists. I cannot bear the smell
of shish kebab or even the Chopin-Let's Kiss
restaurant where you introduced me to sauerkraut
and potato latkes.*

Having finished reading, Michèle politely put the paper
back in the pocket of the coat-sculpture. I wanted to take
off her jacket but she broke away nervously. A brief
silence. Brief, but incisive. Michèle wrote: "Did you really
follow a girl and tear off her coat?" I replied: "Sheer
invention. The madness of art." Michèle smiled. Then
gestured that she had to go to the bathroom. Alone, I
called myself an idiot. Why had I given her that to read?
Sheer pretentiousness. Poetry of despair. I'd written that
text in the midst of an Anna blast crisis. What morbid
desire had driven me to display the most grotesque aspects
of my dearth of love? The piece, without comment, was
dripping with misery. I wanted to bite myself. How could

I live with such a foul, pretentious, sick piece of sculpture? How could I put up with this monster? I cast a cold eye on *Reconstruction of a Thing That Never Happened.* I had an illumination: that thing, dressed up as art, bloated to the third degree of abstraction, gasping, floundering in insignificance, was me. Me: the wreck spat up by Hurricane Anna. I grabbed the coat and threw it against the kitchen wall. The garment, coated with paraffin and jellybeans, exploded, knocking over my assorted spices, my yoghurt thermometer, and the clock that Xenophon had given me. It happened in the time it took to say so and had produced, in the end, a dense and dirty silence. I turned towards the bathroom. Michèle was standing in the doorway. She had witnessed my crisis. I dared not approach her.

Michèle asked no questions. Demanded no explanation. Showed no surprise at my deed of destruction. Just stood in the doorway gazing at me. I was shaken by a surge of love. I loved her. My love overflowed my clothes. Was this the right time? Indeed it was. But I opened the closet, took out a broom, and swept into a pile the debris from *Reconstruction of a Thing That Never Happened.* Ill at ease, I crouched by the trash can where my work, dismembered, lay at rest. Finally, I ventured a look in her direction. Michèle was no longer in the kitchen. I inspected the living room, the bathroom: vanished. She had crept out of the apartment, taking the air with her. I was suffocating. But I got my breath back: I spotted the notepad. Michèle had left it on a chair. Taking refuge under the kitchen table, I clasped it to my breast.

I turned the pages one by one. Taking my time. Rereading those remarks, our tender ping-pong, I savoured our young shared past. Tears blurred my reading. I had been happy with a woman. The proof was in my hands. The more pages I turned and the closer I got to the present moment, the more I felt the despair of a young man curled up under the table in his kitchen who'd been deserted by love. "Did you really follow a girl and tear off her coat?" I reread Michèle's last remark. I said it aloud several times, my voice hushed, to savour all its subtle shades of meaning. How enchanting to give birth like this to a beloved voice at the very heart of my own! There were so many unsuspected things in those few ordinary words. So much crystalline laughter, so much light, so many melodious intonations. How had she been able to hold so much loving material in so small a space?

I turned to the last page. There was nothing on it. Michèle had left me for good. Without an echo.

I lay down flat on the floor. Fixed my attention on the underside of the table, the only sky still available. Examined the damp spots, the knots in the wood, the residue of dried white glue. Figures appeared, swayed. Shadows passed. I was enveloped in fever. The four-letter ghost was smiling. I would never sleep with any girl but Anna, that was understood. Why keep bringing strange women home? Ah, Anna parachute, Anna poppy, one day you'll have no choice but to applaud my persistence. Ah, Anna boat, how could I have destroyed *Reconstruction of a Thing That Never Happened*? How? A hint of raspberry *Mort Subite* rose to my lips. I closed my eyes. My head was spinning. The floor sailed on. Under the kitchen table I drifted off, re-running the "Anna" films, the whole series, on the screen of my eyes whose closed wickets said "Sold Out."

2

Photo Number 36, Roll Number 1

I SAW MYSELF AGAIN developing Anna in black-and-white. Her face, her body, emerged from the developer bath like a wound. I waited for the appearance of her ghost made wavy by the lens the water formed. And so, when she emerged from limbo, I had the image of an Ophelia who, contrary to all expectations, was coming back to life. I grasped the photo as if it were a newborn still wet from the maternal waters, I held it head down to let the water run off, then pinned it to a cord to dry. Late at night, intoxicated by the chemical fumes—the only ones my allergies can tolerate—I went into raptures over Anna's echo which, far from being lost in the dim light, settled into my hideously dilated pupils one photo at a time. When I left the darkroom, love had burned my fingers, my lips, my eyes.

Why had she told me, on the night when I turned twenty-seven, that she could give me no finer birthday present than my freedom? She had decided to kick me out, I had a week to collect my "works," pack them up, find myself another place to live, and disappear from her life. I had become an appendage that she'd sliced off with one swipe. And so, stunned and amputated, I left the second-floor apartment on Saint-Joseph Boulevard, embraced and said farewell to Fred, the huge maple tree that licked our living-room windows on windy nights, then I camped in my friend Xenophon's kitchen until I found an apartment through the classified ads in the *Journal de Montréal*.

Not till I'd settled into my place on Coloniale, my boxes disembowelled, their contents scattered all over the floor, was I able to measure—with the precision given by the sensation that one has been abandoned—the crater hollowed out by Anna's decision. I paddled around in that hole like an insect that has landed on its back. As soon as she heard my voice on the phone, she hung up, efficient as a hammer pounding in a nail with one blow. I was KO'ed for days.

When I finally took delivery of the used fridge I'd bought on Saint-Laurent Boulevard, I rushed over to Xenophon's to pick up my rolls of film. And then I became a bulimic who, by day or night, keeps opening his refrigerator door to gaze upon the food crammed inside, with more saliva than tears in his eyes. In the freezer I'd lined up the small black plastic containers that held the 1080 exposures (30 x 36) of my "Anna" stock that I'd built up over the years. I lingered for ages in the yellow glare that the bulb in the fridge cast over the world, and inspected the miniature regiment of my love, all standing at attention. I developed the films in my collection with the anxiety of a junkie who sees his supply of morphine dwindle every time he shoots up. Anna dose, the road I made you follow, from cold storeroom to cold darkroom, first at the pace of a funeral procession transporting the urns of my love, then that of an archeological expedition excavating from the sand, with cautious little strokes of the pickaxe, the gigantic statue of a mysterious goddess. Roll after roll, photo after photo, from most recent to oldest, my apartment became your mausoleum. For six months I wore myself out, I bled, I diminished from wanting to enlarge you. Only the exorbitant price of photographic paper and the anemic state of my finances could stop your dimensions from expanding.

Something strange happened to photo number 36 on roll number 1. The emulsion, still in the tray, began to sparkle. A spot appeared on the paper, set off one last flash, and went on to trace the outline of your coat. Finally, the complete photo emerged from the white and there you were, Anna beacon, there you were. Your eyes then completed a brief dolly shot and stopped dead on mine. They breathed, they swelled, they squinted, they popped out of their sockets. I rushed out of the darkroom to take refuge under my duvet.

That night I didn't sleep, I was as stiff as an icicle in shock that can't melt and can't gain access to the liquid world of oblivion. I got up in the early hours of the morning and went back to the darkroom, determined to put an end to my stampeding anxiety. Everything was reassuringly normal: objects, odours, and, of course, you, Anna gaze. Naked, shivering, but relieved, I got back into bed with your photo. In powdery slivers, the sun entered through the venetian blinds. Daytime sounds came to me from the lane. I was finally swallowed up by sleep. It was noon when I opened my eyes. I was still holding your photo. I made myself a quick coffee and with my heart on the lookout I studied the final trace of your disquieting photogeneity. I swigged a second coffee to drive away an urge to cry. I went back to your eyes. To what they were regarding.

That was ten years ago. I remembered everything. We were on the beach at Percé, under a gentle rain. Your skin, Anna, registered it only faintly. The subdued sunlight refined the air. I couldn't resist an impulse to take out my Canon which, since we'd left Montreal three days earlier, had just been waiting for the right moment to experience a first contact with your skin. Nervous. Very nervous, I was. Looked as if I'd never held a camera before. And you, Anna, you were excited. For other reasons. It was the first time you'd seen the sea. You only had eyes for the sea. You'd taken off your running shoes and, despite the coolness of the day that was waning behind the ever more numerous clouds, you brushed against the foamy edge of the waves, fraying their fringe with your rapid, cheerful steps. A child. With no embarrassment, no fear. Sixteen years of beauty gambolling in the sound of laughter and the waves.

I'd taken your photo without your noticing. I pressed the shutter as if each click was coming from my heart. You, Anna skin, you performed all the clichéd gestures of happiness: jumping, picking up a pebble, skipping it on the ocean, shaking your hair in the wind, breathing deeply enough to break a rib, valiantly offering your forehead to the sea spray. I took each of your moves as a pose that could only be born of love. You were a poem set free. The rain, so fine at first, was coming down hard. You had rushed away to take shelter in the pup tent we'd just pitched, set back a little from the beach. I was on my way to join you when you came out again, wearing your vinyl coat. You took off again towards the sea without even glancing my way. I called to you. You turned towards me. Click! Photo number 36, roll number 1.

That evening, Anna, in our little blue tent, I'd told you that the Percé beach was infested with vampire bats. You moved your sleeping bag closer to mine. You were blue and beautiful in the dancing light of the lantern. I thought back to these last days: our long bike rides through the little villages, our impromptu campfires, our enthusiastic discussions about your plans to become an actor and mine to become a photographer. Oh yes, life had a reason to exist! Encouraged by that thought, I slipped into your sleeping bag. Your body was wet. It smelled of sweat.

"Anna, do you know what I'm thinking about?"

"Yes."

"What?"

"You want us to do it. Why are you shaking?"

"I've never been this close to you before."

"I don't love you."

"Anna, I'll explode if I don't do it."

"Leave me alone, Christophe! Get back in your own sleeping bag."

"I'll do anything, anything you want if you'll ... "

"Anything I want?"

"Anything!"

"You aren't serious."

"I'll do whatever you want, I swear."

"Eat your bicycle."

"What?"

"Eat your bicycle. After that we'll do it."

"You're crazy!"

"Yes."

Anna zoo, that night I picked up a stone and smashed my bicycle. My teeth were chattering. The wind was nasty, but not as nasty as you. I could hear you laughing behind me. You shone your flashlight on me and it cast upon my act of love a cold light that only the suicidal flight of moths sifted with comprehension. It wasn't the massacre of my bicycle (I called her Eva, she was a Peugeot, I often talked to her) that broke my heart. No! It was your words. As if it were the most normal thing in the world, you told me in detail about how you'd lost your virginity. And I'd thought you were a virgin and naïve! I wished the Gaspé coast would disappear in a tidal wave, carrying with it your voice and the name *Lâm* that you kept repeating. Lâm! Why, Anna, why did speaking that name give you so much pleasure?

Lâm.

3

Little Lâm's Na(t)ive Tongue

Y OUR PARENTS, you told me then, had decided to
become his foster family. In Vietnam, Lâm had
witnessed the massacre of his family. The first time you
saw him he was like a small hunted animal. A survivor. He
was startled by every sound, he never laughed, he spent
hours looking out at the restful and wretched landscape of
Avenue de l'Épée outside the living-room window. As soon
as night fell, he became agitated, his eyes anxious. Your
mother had decided to inculcate in him, a little at a time,
a French that would get him out of tight spots. You, Anna,
you sulked, your face hidden by your grammar book. For
nothing in the world would you have let your mother use
it for the private lessons she gave her little protégé. You
wanted nothing to do with this Lâm! He wasn't the kind
of little brother you'd ordered. He didn't play, he didn't
talk, he barely moved. Everyone surrounded him, cuddling
him, giving him candy, clothes, toys. You life was ruined.

All that changed one winter night. The wind was
wheezing, the snow was sticking to the windows, piling up
against the doors, swallowing the staircase and the gallery
of the house. For the tenth time, your mother told the two
of you to go to bed. You and Lâm had spent all day rolling
in the snow, throwing snowballs, playing bury-the-live-
man, dig-up-the-dead-man. Lâm—unrecognizable in his

winter outfit that puffed him up like an astronaut—had burst the bubble he'd maintained around him for protection. It was the first time you'd played together. Lâm shouted, waved his arms, threw into the new snow his trembling spoken Vietnamese that his choppy French brought down to earth.

Your mother had finally lost her temper and, with a well-aimed smack, let you know that the hour for bedtime had sounded. Lâm scampered to his room like a squirrel that's just spotted a pit-bull. What a strange day! A snowstorm, a new friend, and the smack, the first one your mother had given you. An extraordinary day. The night that followed was no less so.

First of all, you dreamed. You were on a ship. It began to shrink until it was no more than a raft. You were bobbing up and down in the green waves. To keep from seeing them, you lay on your back and stared at the white sky. The sun blinded you. You felt lost. You were starting to disappear when a butterfly alighted on your nose, tickling it. You woke up. You felt something wet between your legs. It was little Lâm's tongue. Anna lethargy, why didn't you call out *Stop, thief!* and kick him? You were a virgin, naïve, innocent, ignorant, at the dawn of pleasure; you played in the snow; you ate candy; your young breasts did not yet wear a bra: in a word, you were a child—spoiled, laughing, healthy, beautiful—and now a little bit of flesh was transforming you into a woman—voluptuous, available, consenting!

The next day seemed to you to pass so slowly. To speed its end, you breathed faster, talked faster, washed the supper dishes faster, did your homework faster, till finally you could announce: "It's bedtime!" Before long, Lâm had joined you. Bolder than the night before, he made you emit sounds new to you, that you stifled with your pillow.

After a week of patient caresses, you were ready to take him in entirely.

Anna's tale was lost in the sound of the surf and the lapping of the foamy water as it vanished on the beach. Dawn was breaking. On the wet sand I could make out the debris thrown up by the night: empty shells, stupefied crabs, chewed-up fish bellies, pieces of flotsam and jetsam. The salty smell of breaking day came all the way to our modest campsite. Ashen-faced, red-eyed, I felt as if I were a vulture floundering in its victim's remains. With a last-ditch effort, I'd been able to swallow a little bit of Eva—a piece of her saddle. It was all I could do. I was just a disoriented lover, dreaming of union with the most charming, the most supple girl on earth. In the light of dawn your eyes sparkled. You were radiant. My bones, my marrow were affected, they produced at a frenzied rate the multicoloured corpuscles of desire that bubbled in my veins. Couldn't you see that it was beautiful, Anna drape, the face at which you were pointing your flashlight, whose light—drowned now in the light of day—was choking like a fish flung out of the water? Surely not. You'd started talking about Lâm's penis, about its petal taste, its ability to slip into you like a tiny icicle of coolness which gentle persistence transformed into a charged battery that could make you levitate! Your voice took on honeyed inflections that gave your words a cruel power of evocation. I was about to flee to escape that torture, when you burst into tears. I held you in my arms. You were crying like a child. Curled up against me, burning hot despite the damp coolness of the morning, you took up your story again, of which your tears had made me guess, quite happily, the sad end.

You and Lâm were no longer content to gorge yourselves with pleasure between the sheets. One of your favourite games was to make love in the places least appropriate for caresses and those most likely to lead to punishment. There were no limits to your erotic pranks. And so you experienced sensual ecstasy in parks, at school, in church, in department stores. But what was bound to happen happened, and when you told me that one Saturday morning, your mother had caught you under the gallery of the house in an extremely compromising and extremely acrobatic position, I couldn't hold back a victory cry that, once it had been expressed, reminded me of the hockey commentators' triumphant, "He shoots, he scores!" The game was over and make no mistake, you had lost. Lâm disappeared from your legs, your bed, your sight, your life—from Montreal too—as quickly as he'd appeared. No one ever mentioned him again. Except that you can't forget the taste of the petal that he'd bared and embedded in your flesh. You were waiting for the day when fate, capricious but honest, you hoped, would make you—during a chance meeting when you were walking or leaving a movie—fall into one another's arms, merging you for life through the lightning strike of a kiss. Your story ended, your damp eyes looked in my direction and you asked me naïvely, with a little half-smile, if a girl like you might interest me. I was breathless and about to collect my oxygen between your lips, which you let me open to the dimensions of my appetite. But you started to laugh and then you ran away without asking for what should follow. I buried my bicycle in the sand, having sacrificed it needlessly.

4

Autumn in New York,
That Brings the Promise of New Love

THE DAY WHEN I WAS LOST in contemplation of your gaze, the one in photo number 36 of roll number 1, I got the idea of devoting a museum to you. Then and there, I jotted at random in a notebook the ideas that were pushing against my forehead. Among the acquisitions essential for the Contemporary Anna Museum, the plans for which I was feverishly sketching, without question the coat you'd worn on the beach at Percé topped the list. I had to have it. My living room, dubbed for the occasion "Vinyl Coat Room," would accommodate it gloriously within its walls. A planned break-in was naturally a must. It would have to be carried out that very evening.

Despite the late hour, Fred wasn't asleep. The maple looked at me with all the roughness of its bark, all the easygoing attitude of its leaves. It seemed to be saying to me: "Pathetic." Saint-Joseph Boulevard, where Anna lived, was deserted. Now and then a car drove by, sucked in by a series of green lights that ran all the way to Mount Royal. I'd put on a pair of pants with a rip in the rear—the only black pair I could get my hands on—and a paint-splattered turtleneck that squeezed my jugular. I hadn't bothered with gloves, taking comfort in the thought that I'd be leaving my fingerprints behind in the world of Anna echo. To give myself confidence, I talked to Fred. I explained to him that if love gave one wings, despair tore them off. Anna had never loved me. Which was her right—and my sentence. I had never accepted the fact that on the day after my expulsion, Anna found nothing better to do than to take parachute lessons. She jettisoned me like some vulgar ballast, then got off on taking off into the wild blue yonder. While I came tumbling down in free fall. During the two years we'd spent under the same roof, this very roof, Anna had started a fire. I burned while I was drying the dishes, doing the week's grocery-shopping, typing her CV for her constant applications for auditions. Everything she had touched, moved, imbued with her fingers, her gaze, her perfume, left burns on me all the more blazing because unpredictable. Finding a hair from her head in the spaghetti sauce made it more piquant. All that, I muttered to Fred, who listened without flinching. When I'd finished I looked up at his highest branches to assess the risks if I were to climb up to the third-floor living-room window. Anna was undoubtedly dreaming. A simple brick wall separated me from her. To get my hands on her out-of-date coat instead of kidnapping her and her dream would be cold comfort, and my plan for a Contemporary Anna Museum was instantly shot down in flames. Fred repeated "pathetic" and sheepishly, I retraced my steps.

I hadn't gone three steps when I heard Anna's laughter. The object of my quest and the subject of all my conversations was roaring with laughter at 3:17 A.M., on the corner of Boyer Street and Saint-Joseph Boulevard! I hid behind Fred, watching for Anna to appear. A couple turned the corner: a man and a woman. The woman wasn't Anna but she was wearing her coat, the same one I wanted to get my hands on for the museum. I dug into Fred's bark with my nails. My dismay seeped into his sap, climbed into his branches, ripped off the last of his red leaves. Who were that man and that woman? Friends of Anna's? They walked past Fred. I saw them disappear into the building. A few minutes later, a light came on in the third-floor window of Anna's living room.

There I was, clinging to Fred's branches, blood dripping down my face. I must have hurt myself during my climb. Fred couldn't help repeating "pathetic." Big deal, I was too busy getting to the branch that looked into the living-room window. The curtain was slightly open. Short of breath, I glanced inside. The unknown pair I'd spotted on the sidewalk were dancing, locked together. I pressed my ear against the window-pane and recognized, with a thrill, "Don't Be That Way," sung by Ella Fitzgerald and Louis Armstrong. It was the first song on a disk I'd given Anna. The woman had taken off Anna's coat and now that my eyes were used to the dimness, I noted she was wearing a dress that belonged to Anna too. Crazy ideas began to sweep over me: Anna was now simply a bundle of limbs cut off with a chainsaw, crammed into a Glad bag, and flung into a dump in the suburbs. Her murderers were there before my eyes. I tried to reason with myself: don't be silly, Anna has sublet her apartment, that's all. She was travelling. Shooting a film, maybe, a commercial, in Europe or even Australia. Without really feeling reassured I went on observing the couple who were now dancing to "They All Laughed." They were embracing passionately. The man was wriggling, his thighs pressed against hers. Ella Fitzgerald launched into the third cut on the disk— "Autumn in New York," my favourite. Her voice sent me deep into a suffocating nostalgia, it made me go limp. I was watching a movie, the tears would come soon, love was triumphant, they kissed greedily, their hands travelled under one another's clothing, their bodies fit the deep, carnal voice that was singing "Autumn in New York, that brings the promise of new love … "; blood was standing out on my injured forehead, my turtleneck was choking me. And then the woman broke away from the kiss to which she'd surrendered, disappeared from my field of vision. The music stopped, then started up again. I realized that she'd just put on a new record.

Another woman singer, but this time the notes sounded as if they were coming from a pair of miniature lips. The words took the form of fine needles of ice that were melting in contact with the air. Vietnamese. I'd eaten at enough ABC combo restaurants (*pho* soup, shrimps and rice, imperial roll, jasmine tea) on Sainte-Catherine Street that I was able to recognize the top tunes from an Asian hit parade. The woman came dancing back, arms raised, making small disjointed movements, like breaking twigs. The man was sitting on the floor and gazing enraptured at his companion's sensual movements. Her long blonde hair looks like yours. I felt almost as if I were ogling your lithe, inviting body. My turmoil grew when the woman took off her shoes and tossed them into the air. The man picked one up and sniffed it, making both of them giggle. Then the woman removed her stockings. She peeled them off as if she were peeling a tasty fruit. I held my breath when she made an elegant move towards the zipper on her dress. How many times had I imagined my hands doing that very thing? The woman had turned around to show the movement of her back. It emerged, naked, unshackled from the garment now gaping nonchalantly on her shoulders, like wings spread half-open. Her serpentine undulations to make the dress fall to the small of her back harmonized with the music, which had just slowed down. A monotonous chant, overtaken by the languorous lament of a flute that spiralled its notes into my inflamed senses.

The woman's shoulder blades protruded, swayed along with her swaying hips, emphasizing the elasticity of her skin to which the soft half-light in the living room added a hint of lovingly rubbed mahogany. The woman stopped moving, stretched her arms, then brought them abruptly to her dress, which was gathered on her lower back, and pushed it down to the top of her buttocks. The man gave an appreciative cry of encouragement that troubled me. The dress slipped down, a little at a time, revealing round, firm buttocks. The man applauded, whistled, shouted to the woman to turn and face him. But she kept her partner waiting—as well as the voyeur I'd become. She stayed where she was, swaying, turned a little to the left, a little to the right, revealing none of the essentials. Then, theatrically, she brought one hand to her hair and in one move pulled it off: a wig! Before I'd even absorbed the shock of that lightning transformation, a second one sent me off balance and I fell: the woman had turned around and displayed the genitals of a man.

Miraculously, Fred caught me two branches down. I straightened up and, climbing from branch to branch, I went back and pressed my red face against the window. Questions had filled my head while it was dangling in space. Who were those two men? A couple of anthropophagists? Had they carved up my tender Anna and were now giving themselves up to these questionable bacchanalia, the better to digest her? In my panic I was sketching the worst scenarios.

Back at my observation post, I heard you laugh. Again! Proof that they'd eaten you! You rose up from their oesophagus in the form of gastric gas, adding to their demented laughter the bright sparkle of your own. They were playing the first record again and I, with stricken heart, heard our favourite song, "Let's Call the Whole

Thing Off." The man, naked, seated, was watching the other one perform. To the sacred words that we'd hummed hundreds of times, he resumed his revolting striptease. He'd already taken off shoes, socks, jacket, and tie, and now, awkwardly, he was unbuttoning his shirt.

I was ashamed. Rather than quenching my thirst for revenge, I stayed in the skin of a voyeur and waited for garments to fall, one by one. Something was soothing my fury, forcing me to witness this ritual to the end. Something was directing my gaze towards this man, who had just turned to strip off his unbuttoned shirt. He reproduced the moves his partner had made earlier, but less elegantly, more nervously. With back bared, he concentrated on pulling the leather belt from his pants, running it back and forth suggestively between his legs before he shed it. He unzipped his pants, which dropped to his feet, revealing blue-striped boxers identical to a pair I'd lost! The man turned around. With a violent thrust of my head I shattered the windowpane and ended up in the living room. There I stood, dripping glass, in front of Anna, whom I'd just recognized as the man in boxers.

My gaudy arrival, noisy and unexpected, set off cries of terror. I myself, deeply shaken, confused, and injured, jumped up and down, spasmodic as a spring, then I tried to approach Anna, who'd taken refuge in the arms of the man who was flinging unknown words, sharper than butcher's knives, at my face. I was torn between joy at finding Anna intact and consternation at finding her in boxers with another man. My own howls only added to the confusion, burying the final vocal exercises of Louis and Ella: "You like potato and I like potahto ... " In her nervousness, Anna had let fall her short black wig. The appearance of her blonde hair, which exploded and was about to run aground on the edge of her naked breasts, nailed me to the rug. Though I cried out my name, it was a waste of time, Anna seemed not to recognize me. I fled, but before I stepped over the windowsill, I picked up her coat from the floor. Then disappeared into the night.

Fred's "pathetic"—he'd seen me take my tumble, head-down—was still ringing in my ears when I landed on the sidewalk. At Saint-Denis I got my breath back. I hadn't gone two blocks in the direction of Saint-Louis Square when I saw a group of four individuals coming towards me. All had on long dark coats and old-fashioned broad-brimmed hats. I couldn't really make out their faces but what I could see was not in the least reassuring. You might have thought it was the living dead. Having spotted me, they approached very quickly and came to a standstill two metres away from me. I dared not move. The smallest one belched. All four came out with a coarse laugh. I decided timidly to join in—a matter of getting along with them. Bad move. They stopped laughing. Gathering up what was left of my strength, I cleared out. They hurled themselves after me like a pack of rabid dogs behind a wounded hare. I turned and crossed the street. I thought I might be able to shake them off if I rushed into an inside courtyard, but my race ended at a brick wall that I set out to climb. In vain. They grabbed me by the ankle and I fell. There I was on the ground, encircled by eight legs. I flung Anna's coat over my head for protection against the shower of boot-kicks I was dreading.

"What do we do with him?"

"I'm hungry and cold, let's go home."

"You don't want to rape him?"

"Too skinny!"

"You?"

"Maybe."

"What do you think?"

"Same as you."

"And what do I think?"

I heard another belch. Then laughter. This time, I didn't intend to join them in their ritual. I played dead. Their laughter stopped. Silence. Tragic. Long. Too long. I couldn't take any more. I decided to risk a glance. I pulled aside a section of the coat and looked through the opening. The beautiful face of a girl was smiling at me with perfect teeth whose brightness contrasted with the flesh of her bare lips. I widened the opening, bringing into my field of vision three more girls, also smiling. They dug around in their pockets and took out some small objects and threw them at me by the handful, running away and singing: *Que c'est beau la vie!* I looked at what they'd thrown. All kinds of candies: Jordan almonds, jujubes, caramels, licorice sticks, marshmallows, honeymoons, Bazooka gum, fruit drops, jellybeans. I even picked up a condom with a wrapper that bore a drawing of a rotten jack o'lantern, grimacing and toothless:

DON'T BE LIKE ME

USE IT

BEFORE IT'S TOO LATE!

I slapped my forehead. I'd chosen to break into Anna's place on Halloween!

My mouth packed with candy I laughed again at my gullibility. I'd been taken in by four girls a lot sharper than I was. As I hurried home, I went on laughing, sounding more and more false, so as not to end up all by myself with a thought that was gaining ground: the man who'd had on the coat that I'd just stolen from its owner at the risk of my life had Asian features: Lâm was back! I burst into my apartment. Undressed. Threw my clothes in the garbage. Took a shower. Idiot, moron, amateur, cripple. I didn't feel good about myself. Why this Halloweenesque striptease, Anna bullet?

After five days of circling around your coat, which lay on the kitchen table like an animal that was dead but rot-resistant, hunger won out over my torpor. I ran outside and gulped down two smoked meat sandwiches with dills, salad, and fries, in a restaurant on Saint-Laurent Boulevard. I knew that after fasting, it was unwise to eat fast and greasy. When the last ketchup-red fry dropped into my gut I expected the worst: cramps, sweat, nausea. Nothing. On the contrary, I felt better. I paid and went directly to a Jean Coutu pharmacy, where you can find just about anything. I left with three kilos of jellybeans. I was thinking about Ronald Reagan. About his intestine. The large one. About the thousands of jellybeans that had been dropped into the presidential gut. I saw again a photo of him that had run in every newspaper of the world a few years ago: "Ronald Reagan's colon cancer." The photo showed the president sitting up in his hospital bed after his operation, surrounded by jars of jellybeans sent by admirers to guarantee a recovery as happy and gaudy as those little bean-shaped jellies covered with multicoloured sugar. The entire world had then learned two things: 1) colon cancer doesn't kill you; 2) the president of the United States was a consumer of jellybeans, big time. Ever since, I couldn't help associating jellybeans with intestines and, in the background, the spectre of a cancerous colon plugged with sugar. I was thinking about all that when I came nose to nose with Ronald Reagan. With his mask. He was looking at me through the holes pierced for his eyes, in a window displaying the most genuine Montreal kitsch.

Amid an assortment of Expos caps, a dusty cowboy hat, a lamp made from a hockey stick, an ashtray sitting on the hoof of a deer or a moose, a collection of key rings, pencils, and coffee cups, sat a row of masks: Frankenstein's monster, Jean Chrétien, live death's heads like those the four girls had worn and, at the centre, Ronald Reagan. The coincidence transformed into necessity the artistic impulse that I'd had in the restaurant a little earlier: to turn your coat into a work of art. I would commit other break-ins at your place and every object I brought home—from the hair on your pillow to the stockings pulled out of your laundry basket—would be the raw material for a work of art that would install in space the weight, the urgency, the intransigence, the enormity of my love. My plan for a Contemporary Anna Museum was taking shape and it promised more than a mere retrospective that would be a boring line-up of the cooled-down traces of your turbulence. That museum would be a kaleidoscope, a kaleidoscope of my passion.

I bought the Ronald Reagan mask and went home, anxious to swing into action. I'd been bombarded with bonbons by some young girls, now I was going to inflict the same treatment on your coat. I sat in the lotus position and told myself: "Concentrate, Christophe. Forget. Create. There are days when everything begins, and there are days when everything ends. Breathe." Impressed by my own words, I picked up the Ronald Reagan mask and put it on. To create "Coat with Jellybeans, Other Bonbons, and Anna Skin," it had struck me as appropriate, if not obligatory, to don the mask.

I set to work by lining up my eyes as best I could behind the undersized holes in the mask. I boiled the coat. The result was disappointing. I stuffed it with old newspapers and left it to dry. Wedged between two chairs, it looked like a scarecrow or a deep-sea diver. I melted some paraffin, painted the whole coat with it, and hurled onto it my three kilos of jellybeans. The work was taking shape. I shuddered, suffocating under the mask which had started to contaminate me. Because without realizing it, I was talking to the coat in English. From my lips came a California accent. *"Yes, yes, jellybean coat, you're gonna be a masterpiece, wait and see. Please, don't look at me like that! Be cool! Trust me! I know what I'm doing. A few more red jellybeans here, a few more yellow ones there and you'll be perfect! Don't worry, honey! I'll protect you from vandalism, I'll give you all my attention, all my heart. You'll be the shining star of this place, O jellybean coat, O Anna sugar with a sweet big A, a sumptuous double* n *and another sweet, cute little* a*!"* Stimulated, frantic, I looked through my drawers for something that would complete my work of art with a flourish. I unearthed an old five-hundred-piece jigsaw puzzle, a reproduction of Rembrandt's "Bathsheba at Her Bath." I thought the subject was apt and I spattered the coat with a big handful of pieces. It lacked white. I added the contents of a bottle of aspirins. The work was vibrating. I waited awhile. Then, with the dexterity of a surgeon removing bandages from a newly operated patient, I freed the coat of its old newspapers. During this delicate operation not one jellybean, not one aspirin fell. I gave some volume to the sleeves, pulled up the collar, and stood it on a stool to serve as a pedestal. "Coat with Jellybeans, Other Bonbons, and Anna Skin" was born. The next day I wrote a brief text that I put in a pocket of the coat. I changed the title of the work. I decided to call it "Reconstruction of a Thing That Never Happened."

A month later, the work was accusing me. I'd done nothing. The Ronald Reagan mask was lying in a corner.

A flaccid little pile. I had no new burglary plan. The plan for your museum, Anna, had deflated again. It was snowing. My windows were dripping with condensation. Outside, the snow on the sidewalks—dirty, grey, trampled, neither earth nor water—reflected my image. One night, I thought I'd spotted you in a yoghurt commercial. I had to watch TV for several days in a row to be sure. Your smiling face was a bright spot in the strawberry costume that covered you from head to toe. It was you, all right. I phoned Xenophon to announce my discovery.

"How about that, it's the Bicycle Eater!"

Ever since I'd told him about my misadventure on the beach at Percé, Xenophon had got in the habit of mocking me by addressing me that way.

"Listen, Xenophon, Anna's a strawberry in a TV commercial!"

"I know. Did you notice the kiwi beside her?"

"Not really."

"You're sure you didn't notice anything?"

"Notice what?"

"The kiwi ... "

"What about it?"

"It's him."

"Him?"

"Lâm. He and Anna ran into each other on the shooting stage. It was during the dance of the fruits. After the banana, the director asked Anna to dance with the kiwi. She fainted. She'd recognized Lâm. They had to take off her strawberry costume and call a doctor. Finally they started the ... "

I hung up before learning anything else. I spent hours in front of the TV. I had to wait till the following day to come across the same commercial. It was true, the strawberry did a dance with the kiwi. I vowed that I'd never eat yoghurt again, with fruit or without. The decision didn't make any changes to the sluggishness that had kept me numb all winter.

Spring arrived with the dandelions. Winter had got me used to seeing nothing on the sidewalks but frozen fish. Now trout and salmon and perches were all wriggling past me, all in shorts and T-shirts. I kept expecting you to turn up at every corner, golden, with a kilometre of dandelions following you like a bridal train. I couldn't stand still. I stank. I was not proud of myself. Basically, you were quite right. You were beautiful, spirited, bold, blonde from here to eternity, you were getting it on with your token kiwi. What could I do to counter that? I decided to be positive. I'd accumulated enough sap during the winter to make me feel like a genius.

In one week, I installed on the walls of the apartment the exhibition "Whatever Happened to Anna?", the fruit of my thirty rolls of film devoted to you. Your coat-sculpture dominated the room. I spent another week writing you a letter of invitation. I failed at making it long. I failed at making it short. I failed, period. Finally I opted for a simple invitation printed on a card. So as not to frighten you, I had slightly modified the title of the exhibition by eliminating your name and replacing it with an ellipsis: "Whatever Happened to … ?" You'd always encouraged me in my photographic work, even saying that while I rarely showed any talent, I was sometimes brilliant. A formulation that was just like you. I invited no one but you, not even Xenophon. I wanted to be alone with you when, moved and mesmerized by the subtle variations in my exhibition, you would shoot me a look of admiration and fall into my arms. If you and I happened to be, for a few moments, within the same perimeter, something would *have to* happen. You never came. The cold buffet I'd put together had become a warm one. Is there anything sadder than food that's sat around too long, waiting for the guest it was prepared for? The rice was pasty, the salads collapsed, the carrots dried out. And my exhibition pointless. Vain. Pretentious. Ridiculous. I threw the buffet down the toilet. I fixed myself an omelette to the tune of "They All Laughed," which I'd bought for myself. Ella and Louis could laugh all they wanted: I cut the Ronald Reagan mask into little pieces and tossed them into my omelette as it cooked.

At the beginning of June, a letter from the Arts Council had saved me from certain hara-kiri: "We are pleased to announce that we are awarding you a grant which will allow you to carry out your project. We hope that ... " The jury had found "interesting and feasible" my proposed "Mayan Stone and Mayan Light: Ruins in Black-and-White." I was taken completely by surprise. In what way was this project more "interesting and feasible" than any other already submitted? Holding the letter, I bowed low to the jellybeaned coat. Expressed my gratitude. It was thanks to its power that I'd obtained the grant, there was no doubt about it. Among the three photos I'd submitted with my application was photo number 36 from roll number 1. I'd retouched it, rebalanced the greys to create a 1950s atmosphere. With my head inside the magic coat—totem of my universe—I dove into the past. I saw again the waves on the Gaspé shore. The scents of the sea, mixed with those of my darkroom, intoxicated me. In a few months I would fly towards other skies, other seas.

Part Two

THE NIGHT OF THE BUTTERFLIES

5

Huachi and Rita

I LANDED IN CANCÚN. The tropical heat of the Yucatán was beating down on me. In the shuttle bus between the airport and town I bought my first Mexican beer. *Cerveza* was the first Spanish word I learned. I had time for two more before I arrived, wobbly-legged, in the centre of Cancún. The bus with its festive air took off in a black cloud of dust. At the reception desk of the Hotel Ana Teresa where I was staying, I was given to understand that the beach was just a few kilometres away. For a few pesos I could get there by bus. I decided that I liked this town, that the country delighted me. Was there any other country in the world where you can buy beer on a bus?

I opened the door to my room with the feeling that I was performing a historic deed. I was launching my trip, my photo project, and, maybe, a new life. The room was pitiful. The smell. A rat had expired there. I opened the window, closed it immediately. It was right on the corner of the hotel, squeezed in between two lively streets lined with terraces where tourists protected themselves from the sun behind enormous pitchers of punch. I took off my jeans—too hot, already wet—and traded them for a pair of cotton shorts. And went outside.

As I explored the area around the hotel, I had the impression that my bare milk-white legs didn't belong there. The sun was setting slowly. I took a seat on a terrace. A waiter came up to me and almost instinctively, I tossed my Spanish for Dummies at him: "¡*Una cerveza, por favor, Señor!*"

My mind had forgotten Anna's existence for more than five hours. An exploit. My trip was off to an auspicious start. I smiled contentedly at the thought that Canadian taxpayers' money was subsidizing my detox cure from Anna. The Mayan project was only a pretext: the time had come to take myself in hand, to get away from her claws. I would go back to Montreal cleansed to the bones. "Out of sight, out of mind," I'd told myself time and again. It was with the fourth beer that I thought about you, Anna light. I was getting slowly drunk to the sound of a mariachi band that had started its act with the first glimmers from the lanterns around the terrace. It was with the seventh beer that I slipped into nostalgia. I was getting old, sitting at the terrace of my memories. The music was listlessly dissipating the mists of my past from which, long ago, your face emerged: a yellowed photo that the creased eyes of the old man I'd become found hard to recognize. Ah yes, little Anna, how I'd loved her back then, she was so charming— that little girl with the firm breasts, with skin like ripe wheat, with a candid laugh, with the perfume of rain. So long ago! With the tenth beer, you were simply a photo faded by my tears, my old man's tears. I stammered your name instinctively. When I got up to go back to the hotel, I had the legs of a centenarian. I flopped onto the damp bed in room 17 of the Hotel Ana Teresa, like a mailbag overflowing with letters that the dream department couldn't sort before dawn. In the middle of the night two blinds snapped open: my eyelids. For a few seconds that lasted an eternity on the meter of my panic-stricken heart,

I didn't know who I was, where I was, who, in the darkness, was shouting that name, that *Anna*.

At seven o'clock I had to flee my room, which was stifling. I couldn't stay still. I wanted to see the sea, to wash myself in its waves. I hopped onto the first bus. Fifteen minutes later, sandals in hand, I was gazing at an infinite tableau: the white of the sand, the green of the sea, the blue of the sky. Those three superimposed strips, washed by the light of morning, were more eloquent than any experimentation in the history of painting. The beach was still deserted. I made a pile of my clothes which I buried in the sand as a precaution, and stepped solemnly into the Caribbean. And came out again, convinced that my heart had been purged, that new blood was reinvigorating my limbs, that I could line up your two sacred syllables, Anna, without going into a trance. No one, when I came home, would recognize in this body worked on by waves, salt, and sun, the Christophe of the gloomy days. Inspired, I wrote in the sand: "fight fire with fire." Only the brutal Caribbean sun would extinguish the fire that Anna had kindled beneath my skin. I'd never understood what pleasure can be had from pretending to be an inert sack while your own skin is burning. Henceforth, my sole aspiration was to take that cruel experiment to the limits of the possible.

Around noon I was alarmed by a cramp. The numerous *cervezas* of the previous day were still at work. My skin was turning red. I reread the statement I'd printed in the sand, to resist the temptation to take shelter in the shade. The cure demanded perseverance. The cramp was churning my stomach, wrenching my guts. I got up. The cramp died down. The sea was sparkling: a blinding mirror I hurled myself into. I swam in the sun. I gleamed like the turquoise carapace of a turtle. I was declaring my happiness when a second cramp made a knot in my bobbing body. I contracted, like a worm. Vomited. Shame, then guilt, grabbed hold of me. Vomit in the sea! I had sullied the planet. Very quickly I gave up these moral considerations. Between two spasms I swallowed some water and lost control of my respiratory system. Waves appeared, in front, behind, and kept me from getting my breath back. Timidly, I outlined a question: "Am I drowning? Not at all, only panicking." I flapped my arms and legs, forgetting the most elementary swimming strokes. I didn't know if I was vomiting or swallowing water. The two actions had merged in a single pumping movement. But which was pumping—the sea or me? I yelled, called for help. Images rushed at one another: Anna giving me a T-shirt for my twenty-fifth birthday; the Percé rock closing around me, suffocating me, my flooded darkroom carrying me off on its acid waves. Anna, always Anna, who, instead of descending, was rising, sucked up by her parachute, disappearing into the sky until she was merely a tiny white dot that was going ...

I got a tremendous punch or a gigantic slap that split my lips and brought my wits back. Near me was a woman.

"How are you?"

"I'm fine."

I wasn't fine at all, but the tone of her question was so kind, so fitting, and the question itself so thoughtful and so obviously not merely polite, given the circumstances, that I decided there and then to forget the torments I'd just survived.

"There's not enough to drown in. See, barely a metre of water."

"Amazing."

"I apologize for the slap. I hurt you with my ring."

"You did the right thing."

She looked at me, surprised and then amused. On the beach she offered me a towel to wipe the blood off my lips. I refused, ran to get my things, wiped myself clean, and came back to sit beside her. She was smoking.

"You don't smoke? A young man like you doesn't smoke."

"Why do you say that?"

"Statistics."

Over her bathing suit she had on a big sweatshirt that concealed her curves. She wasn't beautiful, she was charming. In her forties, at least.

"I didn't react right away when I heard you call for help. Do you understand?"

Actually, no. I assumed an open expression, hoping she'd see that I had some depth.

"I thought you were ridiculous, making all that noise. Before I rescued you I had time to invent a story for you. You have a weird look in your eyes."

"It's the salt."

"You're capable of wit. I was reading when I heard you cry out."

A discreet laugh escaped from the tips of her teeth. She mashed her cigarette.

"The most beautiful sand on the planet, the sand of Cancún. Have you noticed the quality of the grains? All the same, all perfect, all spotlessly white. You could think they were made in a factory. I feel a little guilty, using it as an ashtray. Here, this is what I was reading: *Human Sacrifice Among the Aztecs.*"

I took the book. Shuddered. "Before I rescued you I had time to make up a past for you." Her words still rang out inside me. I handed back the book without opening it.

"The Aztecs made human sacrifices to keep the sun alive. To them, it was a motor. They thought they were protecting it from rust by lubricating it with blood. Let's go now before we burn up."

We'd arranged to meet that evening at a fish restaurant she'd suggested because it was famous for its *huachinango*, a kind of red snapper. Only too happy to spend some more time with her, I hadn't expressed my lack of enthusiasm for its white flesh full of bones and iodine. I spent the rest of the day drinking fruit juice in the shade of the parasols. I was afraid of another cramp.

At the restaurant, I nearly didn't recognize her. She'd got there first. I should have come sooner. Her face disappeared behind a pair of glasses in the shape of a TV screen, with bright red frames that made her look at the same time old and hip. She had on a man's striped shirt, red like her glasses. In a word, I thought she looked awful—while realizing at the same time that there was a good chance she thought the pink-skinned biped making his way towards her looked ridiculous. Once I was seated and bathing in her perfume—something chic, costly, and French—I savoured the pleasure that came with spending an evening in an exotic, romantic setting with a woman. I had an urge to speak your name, Anna, to probe its power over my nervous system. Why tempt the devil?

"I suggest that we don't start by stating our names, professions, disappointments. Let's stay anonymous. I like your gaze. It doesn't say anything, but it lets a person breathe."

"On the beach you told me that before you rescued me, you'd had time to invent a past for me. That's been going through my head all day. I'm curious to know what kind of past you invented."

"I forget. But it doesn't matter, I could make up another one here and now."

There was defiance in her voice. Humour too. We were drinking margaritas. She smoked one cigarette after another. I wanted to take my turn and invent a past for her.

"When you were a little girl your parents forced you to take piano lessons. One day you poured a litre of gasoline over the piano. Then you struck a match. In your Alpine village you became a celebrity. People feared you, but they respected you. At the age of twenty, you won a ski competition. You climbed up the national and international ranks. Your chest was covered with medals. In Austria one day, you had a fall that put you in bed for months. During that time you wrote an autobiography. An immediate bestseller in eighteen languages. You've amassed a colossal fortune that you've frittered away on travel. You came to Mexico to … "

"Go on."

" … to run away."

"That's right. I'm running away from the police. I killed my last husband. As I did the others, for that matter."

"Then I raise my glass to your future victims!"

When the fish arrived we decided to call each other Margarita and Huachinango. By dessert we'd become Rita and Huachi. To my amazement, I'd enjoyed the grilled fish, served with wedges of lime and avocado. Rita was drunk and I was slowly getting there.

"Look at this fish. A head, a long backbone, a tail. It's almost like looking at a hieroglyph or a rebus."

"Or an arrow."

"Which tells you: this way, this is the way life was lived. The fish is a superb animal. It's shaped like a thought that can worm its way into the dullest, the densest, the slimiest brains. The entire life of a fish is spent forcing its way through a crowd. And its smell! More essential, more metaphysical than its taste! That smell goes back to the dawn of time, it holds the secret of matter in gestation. That powerful smell is a key, the only key that can open the gate between us and death. The smell of a fish, its stench, tells the story of the coitus of universal memory, the most brutal impulses and the most refined ones. The smell turns your stomach, the better to turn your heart upside down. A single fish contains the entire sea. It is the flask of time. Take another look at that fish head on your plate. Pitiful, isn't it?"

"Absolutely."

"Actually, no, it's not pitiful, it's grandiose! It reminds us of a thousand other sacrifices. Sacrifice, Huachi, isn't trivial, or comical, or some old thing that worked for the Aztecs and other exterminated peoples. The sun has its followers. And so does the sea. This morning, you could have become a prime victim."

Rita raised her eyes and looked off into the distance from behind her big glasses—beyond the walls, the evening, the hour. The wine had swollen her lips. Her words had moved me. Maybe she'd wanted to take the mickey out of me, but a tear dropped incognito onto my cheek. I was touched. Rita had opened my yes: I had all the characteristics of the ideal victim, about as grandiose as the fish on my plate whose bulging eyes sparkled with compassion for me. I ordered another bottle. Rita emerged from her fog.

"People have written kilometres of learned and fatuous nonsense about the sun's victims. Now, it's true that it hurts to have your chest opened, to have your heart torn out. But it's not just that. Who gets to the bottom of things nowadays? Of course there is the beauty of the deed. Everyone agrees: to offer a heart, your own or your neighbour's, has a certain panache and it's not within the reach of just anybody. Huachi, I can't take any more of this civilization which doesn't acknowledge that a victim is first and foremost the only place on earth where divinity can feel at ease."

"But ... "

"No buts. We have to surmount the slaughter, the litres of blood dripping onto the temple steps, the usual trinkets, and the fetid smell that the first Spaniards found so disgusting. Don't look at me that way."

"What way?"

"You seem lost."

"Rita, you're an amazing woman."

"Please, don't go stupid on me."

"I'm serious. Mexico is nothing compared to what your words express."

"I'd like to bite you."

Anna, the more she spoke, the less I understood and the more she had me in thrall. This evening over a *huachinango* made me see my life in a new light. I felt like getting lost, like walking to the farthest place in my heart, which too often had pointed in your direction and sent me plunging into the void.

When we left the restaurant, Rita couldn't stand up. I wasn't much better. She asked me to find her a taxi. She was staying on the edge of the lagoon. Until we went our separate ways I was waiting desperately for a sign. Did she want me to take her home? Why not go to my hotel? Nothing happened. Sitting in the taxi, she sank into a weighty silence from which only a "*Buenas noches, Huachi,*" could emerge. She seemed to me old, weary, lost. She gave the driver the name of a hotel. The taxi moved off. I looked up at the sky and saw thousands of stars ready to fall onto me. The night was enveloping me in its mystery. I wanted to go to bed as quickly as I could before nostalgia swallowed me up or turned me into a wolf.

My waking was brutal. A lobster opened its eyes. Scalded. My skin cried revenge, tore itself away from my person. Only a small rectangle of my body, drawn in white by my bathing suit, was silent. The treatment had borne fruit. I was experiencing the worst sunburn of my life. I spent the day applying moisturizing cream. I didn't dare go outside. Just one ray of sunlight would have made the highly inflammable material of my body explode. I'd have given anything to be walking on the streets of Montreal, which I pictured as cool, washed by a recent rain. I heard your laughter, Anna.

I went out at nightfall, covered up to the neck. The tourists I ran into seemed abnormally happy. I suspected a conspiracy: they'd all agreed to ridicule me with their smiles—these cotton-clad couples with their skin exuding good health, these youthful high-rollers or seniors at ease with their age. I was the only one who was alone. And so far from you, Anna. Every step, regardless of direction, was taking me away from you. I grabbed a cab. It dropped me off at Rita's hotel. When the receptionist, a man sporting a dark mustache, turned towards me and whispered his "*¿Si Señor?*" I didn't know what to reply, I'd lost all memory of words.

"Just a little *momento, Señor, por favor.*"

That was all I could come up with. I took a tourist brochure from the counter. It was a map of the Yucatán. With an uncertain hand I drew Rita's face. The tip of her chin touched Guatemala and her forehead was bathing in the Gulf of Mexico. I presented it to the man with the mustache, who studied it warily, then suspiciously, then with incomprehension.

"*Una Française, yo* look for *una* woman. *Je cherche une femme* from France. She is staying in this hotel, *comprendo?* I don't know her name, just her face, understand?"

The man smoothed his mustache, seemed to be thinking it over, then disappeared behind a door. He came back with another man, who I realized was his superior from the way he stepped aside to let the other man pass. I launched into my explanations again. This new arrival reeked of a cheap, powerful perfume that tickled my nose and made me sweat despite the air-conditioned lobby. He did something with the map and with his beringed finger, kept pointing to Cancún, thinking that perhaps I was a tourist who'd got lost and most likely wasn't all that bright.

"*No Cancún, Señor.* Look at this face. *Yo* look for this *señora. No conness* her name. She is staying in your hotel, *comprendo?*"

Meanwhile, the man with the mustache had alerted an elevator boy and three housekeepers, who flocked around the map. The youngest housekeeper, a radiant teenager, gave me a look full of compassion. My drawing went from hand to hand, each time provoking more discussions, more shrugs. Without meaning to, I had erected a small Tower of Babel which, like Ravel's waltz, swelled, inflated, and finally carried away dancers, orchestra, and scenery in its giddy round. A small line had formed at the reception desk. A man in an explorer's hat was waiting to be served. I took back the map, re-folded it. I bombarded them with "*gracias, gracias, Señores,*" "*gracias, gracias, Señoras,*" and I was trying to make an exit when a perfectly French remark made me turn around.

"Do you have a problem, young man?"

It was the man with the hat. He had picked up the key to his room and was now heading for me.

"Can I help you? I know the area fairly well."

"No, thanks. You're very kind. I'm not lost, not at all."

"You look as if you are."

"I'm looking for someone."

I opened out the map.

"She's staying in this hotel but I don't know her name. As you can see, I don't draw very well. Perhaps you've noticed her? She's French, like you, I believe, she's forty, maybe more, hard to say, she's not particularly beautiful, she's slender, thin even, she wears glasses, not always, but they're huge, you can't miss them."

"Yes, yes, I know very well who she is."

A sudden burst of hope cooled me. This man was charming despite the hat that made him look slightly ridiculous.

"Do you know where she is?"

"I do, young man."

"I'm lucky I bumped into you."

"Yes, young man, you are."

The tone of his voice had gone up.

"So you know her room number?"

"Yes, young man."

"This is more than I could ever hope for!"

"Yes, young man."

I didn't know how to bring up the burning question. I was more and more annoyed by his "yes, young man," which I was starting to take for a kind but insistent way of laughing at me. Maybe he was a bit "disturbed."

I asked again, "So you know this woman?"

"She's my wife."

I exploded. With laughter. Nervous laughter. A kind of hiccup that left no smudge on the fringe of silence that immediately surrounded it.

"I ... I suppose, sir, that you're wondering why I ... why I'm looking for your wife. It's very simple, I ... I ... I have to ... I've come to ... your wife saved my life, I came here to thank her. I thought that the least I could do was to come here and thank her one last time, I'm leaving tomorrow, you see!"

I rushed to the door but the man caught up with me.

"Young man, why don't we go for a drink?"

The Hotel Caribe had two bars, the Barracuda, which looked out onto a terrace with a pool, and the Mariposa, relegated to the basement, which was dark and covered with frost, the management being so concerned that its clientele not secrete even the slightest drop of sweat. The man asked which I preferred, but without waiting for my reply, steered me towards the Mariposa. On my way down the stairs to the bar I thought back to Rita's whimsical remarks about her putative husbands. And what if she'd been telling the truth? And that this man would be her next victim? Cyanide or rat poison might be at work already. Maybe he'd even collapse on these stairs ahead of me. I took barely a few seconds to come up with that series of zany thoughts and it was with a certain nervousness that I gazed at Rita's husband once we were sitting face to face. A flame flickered peacefully inside a lantern in the middle of our table, tracing a lugubrious shadow on his face. We were the only customers, which was normal given the bleakness of the place. On the other hand, I thought it was not so normal that there wasn't even one waiter to offer us margaritas, *coco locos*, or daiquiris. With all the lanterns glowing on the tables, I felt as if I were in the solemn and pointless emptiness of a church.

"My wife is going to die soon."

I saw a tear run down his cheek. I uncrossed my legs and tried to think of something to say. A waiter appeared out of nowhere and I became absorbed in the list of *bebidas*. I ordered a beer, an Excelsior. Rita's husband ordered a cognac. We were silent until the waiter brought our drinks. Something in the air was lighter now.

"Why her, Lord? Why didn't you choose me instead of her? Why? You can't imagine how many times a day I repeat those hollow questions! And the more I repeat them, the more hollow they seem. But I don't claim to change human nature at my age. Especially not my own. I had to find a word to soothe my anxiety, to give meaning to what is happening. One word, as long as it's the right one, can work its way anywhere, like a tiny flower with its even tinier roots that can pierce the concrete of a wall. And the word was not the word *God*. There's another one that explains, for example, the fact that you and I are here, face to face: fate. I make no claims, young man, to any special expertise or powers that fall under the extrasensory or the premonitory. No, I'm an ordinary man with nothing to hide or feel guilty about. But ... "

His intonation when he uttered that word *but* set off an inquiring gurgle in my guts. He tossed off his cognac and picked up his remark where he'd left it dangling.

" ... but I'm never wrong when fate sends me a signal, when it sends its emissaries. My name is Alfred Leiris, retired engineer. My wife has a tumour on her brain. The specialists give her a few months or a few weeks ... "

"I can't believe it."

"I love her. I know that I won't survive her death. In fact, I married her the better to die with her. We're on our wedding trip. Which will last as long as my wife's tumour allows. My life, our life, now hangs on that small excrescence of flesh making its way into my wife's brain. A flower, you understand, a flower growing ineluctably. Fate."

He ordered another cognac. I hadn't finished my beer yet. I was sorry I'd assumed Rita was an adventuress. I had no heart, no intuition, and I hadn't understood a thing about that woman with whom, I confess, Anna, I had just *fallen in love*. I assumed for myself the word of that broken man: fate. Yes, it was my fate to love Rita, I was certain of it as I watched her husband down his second cognac.

"Young man, love does not give wings. Love amputates: arms, legs. It turns us into quadruple amputees. It drops us like a package on the road, forgets us in the harsh light of day, in the cold rain of night. People, cars, hours, seasons pass—but we, we sink in, we endure. We've decided once and for all not to move, to keep our gazes fixed on some small thing that doesn't concern us. If you only knew how much I love that woman, what a mystery that love is to me, how much I respect that mystery. Fate never sorts things out. It undoes them."

Alfred Leiris fell silent and looked deep into the bottom of his glass. I wanted to tell him that I too was a quadruple amputee and adrift, floating somewhere in Mexico, that love had even made me lose my head, but I merely finished my beer, thinking about what fate had in store for me.

"Young man, I hope you know what you owe my wife."

The abrupt tone in which Alfred Leiris said that put an end to a thought that I'd barely begun.

"She told me about your meeting on the beach. She saved your life. Don't you find strange that coincidence which basically isn't one?"

"What coincidence?"

"That a person who is about to die saves another. That a person whom no one can rescue should rescue another."

I thought as quickly as I could and concluded that it might indeed seem strange. But I didn't understand what Alfred Leiris was getting at. He'd just beckoned to the waiter to bring him a third cognac.

"You leave tomorrow, you told me. Too bad. May I know where you're planning to go?"

I hadn't planned anything and I didn't intend to leave Cancún that soon.

"I plan to go to the border with Belize. Then I intend to travel down the coast."

"All the way to Honduras?"

"Yes, and maybe even further."

"Too bad, young man."

Alfred Leiris looked at me intensely. He repeated his "too bad, young man," took a handkerchief from his pants pocket, and blew his nose without taking his eyes off me.

"You're not insensitive to my wife?"

I acted as if I hadn't heard.

"You're a young man full of passion, that's obvious at first glance. Fate doesn't choose just anyone."

What was he getting at with his "fate"? The turn this conversation was taking annoyed me more and more.

"I'm never wrong when fate goes to the trouble of spending a while with me. You'll excuse me, I have to go back to my room. With all the medication she takes, my wife mustn't be alone for too long. And with all the alcohol she drank with you yesterday ... "

"She told you about that too?"

"Look, young man, don't be in such a hurry. After all, Belize can wait."

He got up, nodded goodbye, took a step towards the stairs, turned around.

"By the way, I don't know your name."

"That's true. It's Christophe Langelier."

"Pleased to meet you, Mr. Langelier."

I got up to shake his hand, but he'd already turned around again (or maybe he was acting as if he hadn't seen me?). I watched him climb the stairs, thinking back to what he'd just said: "After all, Belize can wait." What had he meant by that? I collapsed onto my chair and ordered another beer. I'd forgotten to ask for Rita's real name. But whatever it was, I now knew that she was Mrs. Leiris.

I smiled at the thought that merely three days earlier, I'd been struggling along Coloniale Avenue, worn down, undermined, destroyed by your absence, Anna pearl. What a jump, what a leap I'd made! I had landed at the Mariposa, one lantern among others, and I was burning up my reserves of unloved love.

6

Isla Mujeres

TWO DAYS LATER, a letter was waiting for me at the reception desk of the Hotel Ana Teresa. On the envelope, just my name, hand-written. Violet ink. I was sure it was from Rita. Who else? I hadn't stopped thinking about her. The night before, a bad dream had wakened me in the middle of the night. I was in a meadow, with a rifle over my shoulder, taking aim at a rabbit that was high-tailing it, half-visible in the tall grass. I fired, then ran to the animal I'd just shot down. All I found in the grass was a pair of glasses with the lenses shattered. I heard a branch crack. I turned around. I recognized Alfred Leiris, holding a margarita glass. He had on white slacks and a white shirt.

"Bravo, young man, you got it with your first shot!"

He bent down, picked up something. I went closer. Between his thumb and index finger he was holding a bullet.

"Look at this: the tumour."

"No it's not, Mr. Leiris, it's the bullet from my rifle. Where is your wife?"

Alfred Leiris's glass turned red, overflowed, stained his slacks. I woke up with the thick taste of tomato juice in my mouth.

I opened the envelope. My heart was pounding as I read:

I take the liberty of thinking, Mr. Langelier, that in the wake of our conversation you won't be too surprised to receive this letter. If you are wondering how it was able to reach its destination, please don't think that I have committed any act of espionage. I quite simply asked at the Caribe reception for the address to which the taxi-driver took you when you were made to leave the Mariposa in what I was told was a highly advanced state of intoxication. Or was it sorrow that caused your tears and your delirium? You will forgive me, I trust, for intruding in your private life, but circumstances prompt me to do so.

My wife leaves tomorrow for Isla Mujeres. She will stay at the Hotel Zazil-Há Bojórquez. I'm sure she would be very pleased to meet you there. Do not fear, I shall be staying in Cancún.

It is extremely important, Mr. Langelier, that my wife not know about this letter or our meeting. You will certainly understand that her condition does not permit us to take any risks regarding her emotional reactions, if I may put it that way. In fact, to be frank, my wife's condition is deteriorating. I am afraid that in a month's time she will leave us. As I have told you, I will not be able to bear it. But that's another matter and I don't want to burden you with it. On the other hand, I have no doubt already shocked you with this letter. I can hear you saying with surprise: What an unscrupulous man! He pushes me into the arms of his wife; can there be a worse depravity? I grant you that. I am perverse. And I shall be prepared to do much more, even if it should only last one second, to bring some happiness (or pleasure, or relief—call it what you will) to my beloved wife.

I won't try to hide it: at my age, I cannot claim to any sort of prowess. Which is perfectly banal and I blush at having written it to you. But for a while now my wife's appetites have increased considerably. Abnormally. The doctors had warned me that shortly before the end, a fresh energy would shake up her poor body. Sad fireworks for a wedding trip, I'm sure you agree. I feel guilty, a thousand times guilty, at my inability to bring her those last moments of ecstasy. Can you, Mr. Langelier, feel even a thousandth part of my agony?

Before I leave you, I would like to remind you that my wife saved your life. That fact does not oblige you to do anything, but in my humble opinion it has united your two destinies irrevocably. When I saw you in the lobby of the Caribe, Mr. Langelier, before I even spoke to you, I sensed that you were someone out of the ordinary. You will, I trust, put a little faith in the old man who is writing to you now.

P.S. If your own fate has already taken you onto the road to Belize, I will have written into the wind!

Alfred Leiris hadn't signed the letter. I was sniffling. I'd been crying. Never in all my life had I been witness to a love so pure. Once I'd finished reading I was deeply in love with that man's love for his wife. A love, Anna ricochet, that cast a shadow over the love that I'd lavished on you and from which I tried with all my might to exclude myself. So much so that I was assailed by doubt: had I loved you *enough*? Wasn't I on the wrong track here in this room at the Hotel Ana Teresa? Shouldn't I instead use the distance of the journey to measure the road I still had to cover if I hoped to attain true love, the love that would carry me away in its wake and fulfill us mutually?

I reread the letter. I thought it strange that Alfred Leiris should see himself as an "old man." He hadn't seemed it to me. Now, though, he had convinced me: the man whose life Rita had saved was someone out of the ordinary.

I opened my guide to the Yucatán and looked up Isla Mujeres in the index. I learned that it was a small island, barely four kilometres wide. The poetic-touristy style of the guide described it as a delightful seaside resort, a floating emerald surrounded by coconut groves, fringed with fine, nearly-white sand created by the disintegration of coral reefs that were in turn described as veritable sea gardens where thousands of luminous fish spent their vacation. But what drew my attention, excited my imagination, and reinforced me in my intention to go to the surprising rendezvous engineered by Alfred Leiris was in the last lines that described the island. I read that Isla Mujeres meant "Island of Women." Alfred Leiris was right. Something was on its way. A ship had been launched. I was on deck and it was impossible for me to disembark or to retrace my steps. I was sailing ineluctably towards Isla Mujeres. I, Christophe, who'd always thought that fate was limited to characters in novels, was discovering that I had no reason to envy them.

I went on with my reading. The guide told me again that the name of the island had come from an observation by Francesco Hernández de Córdoba when he landed on its shores in 1517. Most of the temples he discovered there were dedicated to feminine idols, fertility goddesses. My over-excited mind needed nothing more to adorn Rita's head with a divine halo and grant obscure powers to her tumour, that statuette plunged into the depths of her soul. When I closed the guidebook, I was overtaken by a terrible attack of nerves.

The next day, I boarded the ferry at Puerto Juárez. An absurd happiness lit up my eyes, giving an exquisite sweetness to the breeze that was ruffling my hair. I was radiant. Watching on the wharf for the ferry to arrive, sitting on my suitcase, I filled my lungs with the fresh morning air. Sea air—a mixture of salt, fish, kelp, rotted beams, motor oil, and adventure. When my gaze slipped onto the green mirror of the water, I felt an irresistible urge to live, to bite, to forge ahead. That morning, I'd packed my bags, ordered eggs and coffee, paid my bill, taken a taxi to Puerto Juárez, sensing that I was doing some deeds that were perfect, beautiful, harmonious, linked together with the grace of a dance. I had sworn to myself, when I saw the ferry approach, that from now on everything I embarked upon would be marked by lightness. I was all decked out for adventure, sails taut, and your name, Anna, had a new taste, a taste of mint. I confused having a destiny with being made of the stuff of heroes for whom adventure is simply their daily lot. Christophe Langelier was not just anyone! I was even convinced, Anna— surrounded by suitcases, dressed in shorts, skin tanned, Canon slung over my shoulder—that I was handsome.

From the shore we got a glimpse of the flattened mass of Isla Mujeres. I was disappointed. My heart was beating to accompany a liner launched onto the seven seas, not a ferry that shuttled back and forth a dozen times every day. But the photographer's instinct stirred in me and despite my reluctance to frame my shots in tourist areas where the ghosts of thousands of clicks could still be heard, I snapped a few of Puerto Juárez disappearing into the sea spray. Then I turned my attention to the Island of Women. Soon I could make out the dark and swaying heads of the palm trees, the pink and grey of the hotels, the bright spot of shirts or skirts twinkling on the coastline. The closer the ferry got to the island, the more tangible Rita's presence became. I'd spent only a few hours with that woman but I was behaving now like a soldier going to meet his beloved after an endless war. And instead of laying down my arms, I was brandishing them. My own war was beginning. I'd drawn up a plan of attack. With my feet on the ground, I was off on a mission. I would surpass myself. My passion would bring Rita more than "relief." My passion would pass through the secret currents of her flesh, it would go to where the evil began, curb it and annihilate it. I would bring her the treatment of a shock of love.

When the ferry's motor stopped, silence shrouded the universe. My heart paused. Very briefly, but long enough to grasp what was happening to it. I could see clearly. My focussing had never before been concentrated so well on a single image, clear and quick, the superimposition of Anna that had scrambled my life. I was about to perform an energy transfer. That which I'd accumulated over the years was about to burst the sky. In the midst of a giddy round of ideas and sensations, I was visualizing a geyser that would dislodge, pulverize Rita's tumour—and my love for Anna. I was so troubled by the vision that I reflexively got to my knees the moment I was on the island soil, a veritable Christopher Columbus discovering the paradisal Indies, a realm that smelled of love and spice.

Staying at the Zazil-Há Bojórquez was out of the question. I contented myself with the modest Rosario, a simple two-storey hotel painted a cheerful blue, very close to the pier that I'd just left. It had a view not of the sea but of a tiny inner courtyard where yellow cats caught flies in the dust. A bird cage, empty, floated in the air. A small wicker table flanked by a white plastic chair had been positioned out of the sun. I sat there sipping a lemonade. The sensation of lightness with which I'd awakened hadn't left me, but I found it impossible to make up my mind to call Rita at her hotel or to go there directly. I couldn't quite imagine myself knocking on her door and saying: "Hello Rita, I was in the neighbourhood and I was wondering if you'd like to spend the evening together!"

For a moment I was lost in contemplation of the yard. I found it attractive despite its small size and its sorry state. It was a painting, a poem, a symphony. I was part of it in the same way as the table, the walls, the cats. I got up from my chair without thinking and made my way over to the birdcage. Rusted iron. Small black droppings, dried. A green feather. Who knows? Could the cats have devoured the bird? A parrot, most likely. I stuck my hand inside the half-open door and picked up the feather. It seemed to me that all the years I'd lived had gone by only to bring me to that cage and that single green feather. My life had been a labyrinth. I'd just come out of it and, without knowing how or why, I was emerging into this courtyard lost in the heart of an island that was itself lost in the Caribbean Sea. I realized that I'd come to Isla Mujeres to become a man. Why had I thought that the cats had eaten the bird? It had freed itself from its cage and now it was flying!

I set out to explore the island. At the corner of the first street after I had left the Hotel Rosario, I stumbled upon a little shop that rented motorbikes. A young boy button-holed me immediately. I'd never driven a motorbike. I let myself be easily convinced by the boy who, in five minutes, and in Spanish, gave me a driving lesson. He took my deposit, then handed me the keys and left me for another customer he'd just spotted. I hadn't understood a word of his explanations. I gripped the handlebars, turned the handles: right, the gas, left, the clutch. Or was it the other way around? The main thing was knowing how to use the brakes. When I turned the key, when I heard the first backfiring, the back of my neck stiffened and a new strength steeled my gaze. Between my thighs, the motor rumbled. If only Anna could see me now, I thought, releasing the brakes for the first time!

I headed for the port. I wanted to get away from the busy streets. I reflected that since I was on an island, I couldn't lose my way. I set off aimlessly. I followed the shore, looking straight ahead. The road left the coastline, veered off slightly inland. I was perched on a motorbike and I was entering the jungle! The wind touched me with the sweetness of a caress, the warmth of human breath. Never had I felt so free, so happy, so intrepid. The road zigzagged between the coconut palms and the rocks. I thought I was flying. Tears multiplied my vision. Light, light as the parrot's green feather! I speeded up, squinted to get a better view of the landscape slipping away, reduced now to a luminous jumble of colours. Only stains. Stains of green and stains of sky-blue. I speeded up again. The ghost of my bicycle visited me. I hadn't mounted anything with two wheels since the night on the beach at Percé when I'd dismantled my beloved Peugeot. I was crying Eva's name at the top of my voice when, after an acrobatic turn, the sea came into view in the distance. I braked in a cloud of dust. I got off the bike and made my way, bow-legged, towards a small promontory.

Only a god could gaze upon such beauty without trembling. The sea sparkled, ablaze. The silence shattered its surface into lozenges of gold and emerald. Two white sailboats were gliding towards infinity, etching a line of foam beneath their hulls. I had just discovered eternity. I sat on the ground. Got up again at once. It was scorching. I leaned against a big rock, let my gaze drift towards the horizon. A small animal scampered away between my legs: a lizard. He'd come to a standstill a few metres from my feet. I got down on all fours. As silently as I could, I advanced in that position towards the animal. In his jaws he held a butterfly that he was tearing to shreds, making snapping sounds. The butterfly's wings, spasms of blue and yellow, disappeared by fits and starts into the raw green of the lizard. A sense of urgency swept over me. I jumped to my feet, making the reptile run away. I had to find Rita at once. Every second counted. My adversary did not rest, was advancing millimetre by millimetre towards its ultimate goal. I understood what my presence on this island really meant. It meant saving Rita from *death*. I hopped onto my bike. I had to get moving, at once. I'd burned my butt on the sun-heated saddle. I pushed the bike towards the big rock where I'd sat, the only spot in the vicinity that offered a little shade. I climbed onto the rock, from where I could see that I was only a couple of kilometres from the tip of the island. On the farthest point stood a temple, no doubt one of many dedicated to fertility, as I'd read in my guide to the Yucatán. I decided to go there. The present time was a conveyor belt. I just had to let myself go. I looked down at the bike, christened it Adamo. This bike was one of the numerous pieces that were set in motion by my fate. It merited a name. I went to check the condition of the saddle. The leather was still hot. I breathed out, clapped my hands. Convinced of the futility of my attempts to cool it down, I took off my shirt, draped it over the saddle, and got back on the road, swaying dangerously from cheek to cheek.

A few minutes later I parked in the shadow of a minibus stopped at the end of the road, fringed here with sand and brushwood. On its door, in big letters, was printed "Zazil-Há Bojórquez": Rita's hotel! She was somewhere around here, I was positive.

I climbed up the slope and very quickly came to the summit of a small plateau that opened onto the void. A jumble of ruins ran along the precipice. A dozen individuals were listening to a guide. A young man was taking photos with a Polaroid, perched on the remains of a staircase overgrown with weeds. No sign of Rita. I moved, unseen, to a stone column whose blocks lay dismembered on the ground. I could hear clearly the explanations of the guide, who was speaking French with a Spanish accent. I peered at the women's faces. Sweat was running down my forehead.

"There are several hypotheses. There are always several hypotheses. Because the temple was built on a cliff at the end of the island, it's thought that it may have been used as an observatory. On that point, there are three hypotheses: *Uno*, the observatory collected meteorological data; *dos*, the observatory collected astronomical data; *tres*, the observatory collected both kinds of data. Recent digs have suggested other hypotheses. As I told you, there are always a number of them. Now, if you would follow me."

The guide, surrounded by a bubble of mystery, made his way towards the edge of the cliff. The group very sensibly followed him. The young photographer got down from his perch and joined the others. I came closer, gliding along the blocks. I could hear the sound of waves.

"The excavations began not on the temple site, but here!"

In a theatrical gesture, the guide threw his cigarette over the end. All heads leaned forward at once towards something that I couldn't see, but imagined to be an abyss. A woman in her sixties stepped back, saying that she suffered from vertigo. The guide, pleased with the electricity that had put some tension in the air, went on with his explanations.

"Observe if you will the rock face that starts here and goes to the shore down below. Stand at an angle, like this, and take a good look. What does it remind you of?"

A moment's silence transfixed the group. Then the bravest members leaned over and examined the escarpment. The guide smiled, inspecting the faces at work.

"An eagle!"

It was the young photographer who had just cried out. The guide applauded.

"Bravo! There was a German archaeologist who, after noting that the cliff resembled the profile of an eagle, started digging on the shore."

I wanted to leave my hiding place and ask him why the archaeologist had come up with such an idea, but the young man did it for me. In a dramatic about-face, the guide turned and held out one arm, which the group followed with their eyes as if it were a single head.

"Look down there. You can make out the steps of a staircase leading to the temple entrance. A platform had been set up where the victims were immolated on a sacrificial stone, then thrown to the bottom of the stairs— after their hearts had been torn out. The name of the sacrificial stone was *quauhxicalli*."

The guide paused, then repeated: "*Quauhxicalli*, which means ... "

"The Eagle Stone."

It was Rita who answered the guide's question. She had emerged like a divine apparition from the pile of stones in front of the remains of the staircase. She had on a straw hat that plunged her face into shadow. The guide went over to her and the group followed immediately. He bent down at her feet.

"Here, exactly under your feet, there was a broad flat stone. It still exists. You can see it at the National Museum of Anthropology in Mexico City. On that point there are several hypotheses. *Uno* ... "

The guide went on with his explanations, but I couldn't be bothered to listen. My heartbeats were burying them. I kept an eye on Rita. That woman, so upright, so proud, was going to die. Nothing in her appearance gave any sign of it. In the face of such courage, I felt my own diminish. My rescue attempt struck me as disproportionate, aberrant. What arrogant logic had led me to think that what I called idiotically "my love" could hold the antidote to a tumour that the most sophisticated medical hardware couldn't even scratch? Lightness had just abandoned me. I was about to go back to the hotel, intending to leave the island as quickly as I could, when I saw the group move towards the edge of the cliff again. I could even see Rita's face. I sensed beneath her adult features the little girl she had once been. I could see a little saliva stuck between her lips. Strange Rita. What was her real name? Juliette? Anaïs? Ruth? Claire? Monique? Whatever it was, I thought to myself that Rita suited her best. She was talking to the guide. Again, I listened.

"So the cliff was sacred?"

"On that point there are two hypotheses. *Uno*, the temple was considered to be the extension of the cliff; *dos*, the cliff was considered to be the extension of the temple. But both hypotheses lead to the same conclusion."

"Meaning?"

"The victims were thrown off the cliff. Eagle Cliff, as we believe it was called, formed a gigantic natural staircase. Which was why the German archaeologist had the idea of starting his excavation at the foot of the cliff. By digging down ten metres, he found what he was looking for."

"Another *quauhxicalli* stone?"

"Not at all, young man."

"The victims?"

"That's right, *Señora*. The archaeologist unearthed hundreds of skeletons. Expert appraisals showed that all the skeletons were those of young men. Now, if you would follow me."

I was furious. During the guide's last explanations, Rita and the young photographer hadn't stopped flirting. They'd gone from discreet wink to furtive touching. The guide had led the group to a pillar covered with inscriptions. They were too far away for me to make out their words. Several were crouching around the monument. Rita had offered a cigarette to the young photographer, who'd accepted it. Which drove me crazy. I could still hear her telling me on the beach: "You don't smoke? A young man like you doesn't smoke." But she hadn't hesitated to offer a cigarette to this beardless, long-haired youth who handled his miserable Polaroid like a one-armed blind man. What did she think I was? A child? An incompetent?

I stomped off towards the bike, fists clenched, seething with rage: "She's flirting with someone who could be her son! She's going to breathe her last in a matter of minutes and all she can think about is encouraging callow little boys to smoke! And on top of it all, she's married! She's on her wedding trip! Anna, Anna, can you imagine anyone more naïve than me? I'd been on the point of giving her all my love. Very well, I'll force it on her. Why should I bow before a teenager who's just discovered that John Lennon was one of the Beatles? He wears his hair long to hide the empty space behind his forehead! Alfred had warned me. Shortly before the end, Rita will be plagued by violent desires. I have proof of it. The end is nigh. Time to get moving."

Without catching my breath I started the bike. I managed to climb the narrow strip of pebbles that led to the archaeological site where, wreathed in a cloud of noise and dust, I made my appearance. I searched for Rita's eyes. The group of tourists was still massed around the pillar. I was humming in the dry air, radiating as if my body were wearing a suit of pure and polished armour made of shining metal. At least that was the impression I had when I spotted Rita flanked by the boy with the Polaroid. They'd gone back to the top of the ruined staircase. Rita was standing on the site of the Eagle Stone, smiling at the boy as he took her picture. I gripped the handlebars as if they were the horns of a bull. I stepped on the gas, hard. The bike screeched, ploughed into the ground. All eyes turned towards me. In spite of the speed, in spite of the white light of the sun that was overexposing the landscape streaming by, my overcharged brain recorded the slightest details that came to it from my eyes. I could see very clearly the guide waving at me to stop. I couldn't make out his words but on his face I saw astonishment, then stupefaction. I saw the group of tourists scatter for protection behind the blocks of stone. I saw that Rita, her hand shielding her eyes, did not recognize the man she'd saved from drowning in the energetic silhouette of the biker who had just offered her his love. As proud as a young god, I was about to brake at the foot of the ruined staircase when the bike reared up. My shirt tail had got caught in the rear wheel. The bike raised itself up with such power that it threw me to the ground. It went on rolling and hurled itself, with the determination of a kamikaze pilot, into the void. For one brief moment it floated in the air, then it crashed. I fainted before I could hear it shatter against the rocks on the shore.

7

A Cemetery in the Sand

THE NEXT DAY, when Rita came to see me at the Hotel Rosario, I was drinking a Corona in the little inner courtyard and I had a brace around my neck. There was a parrot in the cage now. A hideous loser of a parrot who kept repeating, non-stop: "how-do-you-do-very-well-thank-you-and-you-how-do-you-do-very-well-thank-you-and-you ... " Where were the cats when we needed them?

I had spent the night in the clinic on Isla Mujeres. I'd just fallen asleep when a nurse woke me up and gave me to understand that I could go back to my hotel. It was dawn. I was shivering. All night, I'd thought I was dying. Staring, watchful, I'd kept an eye on myself, reviewed the pain in my joints—my way of counting sheep. My body seemed to be nothing but a soft envelope filled with a hodgepodge of broken bones. A fan near my head was as noisy as a helicopter. There was no window. I felt as if I'd been relegated to the most sordid section of a disused morgue. The smell of fried fish and disinfectant came to me through the partly-open door which let in a yellowish light that leaked onto the floor. The diagnosis was clear: I was going to depart this life on Isla Mujeres. This was not the time for slumber. I didn't want to die in my sleep, slipping towards death like a carefree rock being sucked in by quicksand. I would prefer, Anna slab, to use the time I have to imagine your quivering lips when you hear my death announced. Through the lens of anxiety I examined the corners of your eyes, to catch the gush of your scalding tears. I saw you jump from a plane, harnessed to a black parachute, taking your grief for me into the sky above Montreal. I fell asleep in the sweet monotony of your infinite sorrow, in the soothing procession of your afflicted faces. How I loved you, Anna, that night.

After I left the clinic, where I'd thought I'd be spending the last night of my life, noting that the Caribbean sun had also risen for my damaged little self who was ambling down the deserted streets of Isla Mujeres, I was struck by a brutal happiness. I stretched my aching arms and breathed in the fresh morning air. Lightness! Lightness is green! Singing those words, I was on my way to the Hotel Rosario, savouring every footstep, every breath of air, seeing as beautiful every piece of garbage stuck between two flagstones, every storefront, every restaurant sign, stunned that so much beauty could accumulate around me.

Back in my room, this morning euphoria was turning to despair before the image sent me by the bathroom mirror. I was starting to miss the cocoon of fever and confusion I'd simmered in, lying on the narrow bed in the clinic. As I studied my swollen face, my glassy eyes, the previous day's events came flooding back, imposing themselves on my mind: I had rented a motorcycle, I'd christened it, and I'd sent it into the void. I got into bed and hid between the sheets. Poor Rita! How would I be able to save her now? I was certainly going to jail. I would die incognito, bitten by infected rats. Rita would also die.

The phone put an end to my moaning. It was Rita. She'd found out that I had gone back to my hotel, out of danger. She offered to come and see me. She had called the clinic every hour for word about how I was doing. When I hung up there were tears in my eyes. In spite of her own condition, Rita had gone without sleep last night, so she could get word about the minor casualty that was me. I splashed cold water on my face, gulped three aspirins, put on clean jeans and a long-sleeved shirt to hide the bruises on my arms, went out to the little courtyard, ordered a Corona, and waited for Rita, fixing my mind on the parrot's "how-do-you-do-very-well-thank-you-and-you."

When I saw her arrive, I felt a surge of love in my veins. I was seeing her in a dress for the first time. It was made of an exuberant print, all intertwined flowers, ivy, and butterflies. She'd pushed her hair behind her ears, drawn a faint line under her eyes with blue pencil. Before I had time to get up and greet her, she was standing right in front of me, offering me her face with its smile brimming with mischief. She dropped a cool kiss on my forehead, inspected me, then got the giggles—which made the parrot go berserk. He bounced around in his cage like the bead with the winning number on a TV lottery.

"Can you walk?"

"Of course!"

"Then let's get out of here!"

She grimaced at the orbiting parrot, took me by the hand, and dragged me along, laughing. It was the first time I had touched Rita. Her hand was warm and slightly damp. I couldn't come up with a single intelligent word. Whatever I had in my head was reduced to "How do you do, Rita?" I resigned myself to letting her lead the way through the sun-flooded alleyways. From the speed of her walking, I deduced that Rita knew where she was going. We walked up a pedestrian street decked out with bunches of T-shirts and necklaces made of pink shells. With every step I took I felt a shooting pain inside my skull. I thought again about the labyrinth. For wasn't I, with Rita's firm hand guiding me, in the process of finding the way out? Something wonderful, something irrevocable was about to happen in my life.

We very quickly left the tourist centre. Around a corner we found ourselves in the middle of nowhere. In a sizzling bubble of silence, Rita slowed down. We were walking on a broad, yellow street covered in sand. On our left was a wall. The silence of this street was quite simply the sound of the sea coming to us from the other side of the wall. The tip of the island, one of its countless tips, was nearby. Rita seemed happy, elastic. She wasn't walking now, she was floating. I was looking at our two shadows, short and black, which the midday sun was casting onto the flagstones. Rita pointed to a cat on the roof of a house. He seemed all alone in the world, the astonished survivor of a global catastrophe. Where had all the people gone? All the T-shirt-buying tourists? I looked at the blue and dusty windows of the houses. I was hoping to glimpse behind the curtains a head, a forearm, a gaze. No one.

"Not too tired?"

"Not at all!"

I was lying. This race through town had left me dehydrated.

"I had the fright of my life. Look."

She'd taken a photo from her purse. I studied it, glad of the pretext for standing still.

"Is that me?"

"You give off a scent of tragedy, but when I look at you, you make me want to laugh."

"Who took this photo?"

"Someone. A lucky coincidence: you fell into his frame like an acrobat into a net."

The photo was startling. It had obviously been taken less than a second before the impact. In the lower right-hand corner you could see the tip of the bike's handlebars. The rest of the frame was filled with my body being hurled into the air. My head disappeared into the upper left corner.

"Everyone thought you were dead. You'd stopped moving. Andy gave you the kiss of life."

"Andy?"

"Andy. The one who took the photo."

"You know his name?"

"What's wrong with that?"

"Nothing. No, no, nothing. So he gave me ... "

" ... the kiss of life. You opened your eyes. You looked at Andy. You wanted to kiss him. The whole group from the hotel was watching. When Andy stepped aside you mumbled a name, then you started yelling, 'Don't leave me!' and poof, you fainted again. They carried you to the minibus. You were delirious the whole time."

I had folded the photo in four and stuffed it in my mouth. A wave of acid flooded my throat, I scraped my gums on the sharp edges of the plastic, but I went on chewing this amateur snapshot. When I managed to get it down, I realized that the kid with the Polaroid may have saved my life. A wave of guilt unfurled from my belly to my lips. The photo resurfaced. I spat it out, piece by piece. Rita grabbed my hand and led me away. We started to run along the low stone wall. The sun was kindling a trail of powder on the shards of bottles planted in its crest. Rita pulled me towards an entrance. Without realizing it I'd just passed through a gate into a cemetery.

It could be seen as a miniature city buried by a sandstorm so that only some gables and dormers were visible. Or a lunar beach where small blind boats had washed up over the centuries. Instead of paths, there was a muddle of tombstones and blue or pink niches. Rita wove her way between the graves, waking the sand from its lethargy. She took me to the statue of an angel whose right index finger, placed on its lips, was saying "ssshhh!" while the left one, sure of itself, pointed to the sky. Rita pulled off her sandals.

"Sand, sea, death. With your neck brace you're as stiff and dignified as this angel. Come closer. Don't you think there's a resemblance? Your nose. Turn around. You have a Greek profile of rare audacity. Not even the slightest little bump. A perfect bridge. Do you know what I'm thinking about?"

"I never know what you're thinking about. You're too full of life."

"I'm thinking that your neck brace gives you a lot of charm."

I turned red. Rita was letting sand run between her fingers. Was she thinking that her death was nigh?

"Why did you do that?"

"Do what?"

"Swallow the photo."

"It was just nerves."

My reply had led to a theatrical silence. Rita went on playing with the sand. She was sitting on the corner of a tombstone, a long paved slab inlaid with a ceramic book. On the left-hand page, a name and two dates had been carved. On the right-hand page, a little ship—the kind we made as children by folding paper—was floating on waves that had been drawn with a few lines. Above its sails undulated these words in gold: *siempre vivirás en nuestros corazones*. At the base of the book stood a small niche of very pale blue.

"This sand makes you want to swim in it. The dead in this cemetery are seashells. Place your palms gently on the sand. Feel the work that's going on underneath. Flesh doesn't rot here. It is transformed into coral, into mother-of-pearl, into infinite spirals, sparkling conches."

I understood why Rita had brought me to this place. She was already seeing herself underground. She was here at this sand-covered cemetery edged by the sea in order to come to grips with death. I threw myself at her with all the passion of which I was capable under the circumstances, to cover her with kisses as blistering hot as the sand. She was so surprised at my behaviour that she jumped to her feet. I missed my target and collapsed full length, my nose on the book's little ship. I wished I could disappear into its pages, pass through it, bury myself kilometres underground. The smell of a cigarette brought me up to the surface. Rita, standing upright, was smoking.

"Get up. Come closer."

I obeyed like a robot. She looked deep into my eyes.

"I suppose that was another nervous reaction."

"Rita, I want you."

Anna vestige, I swear that Rita's eyes opened so inordinately wide I could see her anguish fluttering deep inside her. I threw myself at her again. Our bodies rolled in the sand among the graves and the dusty crosses, the lanterns and the salt-eaten flowerpots.

I wanted to take off my jeans. I would give her everything. My love would save her. Just as I was about to accomplish that miracle, I was hit on the head. I sank into nothingness. When I came back to myself an angel was staring at me. I brushed away the sand that was stinging my eyes. I looked again: yes, I had seen an angel. I concluded that I was dead, in heaven, and to my great disappointment, not happy in the least. My head hurt too much for me to appreciate this impromptu paradise.

"Huachi, Huachi … hou … hou … "

The angel was speaking to me even though its lips weren't moving.

"Huachi, hou … hou … are you all right, can you hear me?"

I pulled myself up by leaning on my elbows. I was not in heaven. Rita, sitting across from me, was holding the angel's head in her lap. I raised my own head. Just above me, I could see the statue's decapitated body.

"I said that he looked like you."

"Who?"

"Him."

Rita pointed to the angel's head. She was crying.

"You have the hardest head I know."

Her silent tears flowed more copiously. She was a different woman now.

"I have so many things to tell you."

The sea nearby was rumbling. Rita held the angel's head against her stomach. She'd probably wanted to talk about her illness. I was about to say, "Don't bother, Rita, your husband told me everything," when she gave me a determined look.

"Can you turn around?"

"Sorry, what did you say?"

"I'd like to show you something. Just behind your back."

I was leaning against the base of the statue. I turned around.

"Can you read the epitaph?"

I swept aside the sand that had accumulated on the stone slab. Little by little the gilded letters stood out. I stepped back to read more comfortably: "An angel has flown away." It was written in French. A name had been engraved above the sentence. I could only see the upper part of the letters. I plunged my hands into the sand and uncovered the entire base.

ALFRED LEIRIS

That was the name I'd just exhumed! What was Alfred Leiris doing in the cemetery on Isla Mujeres? Had he quite simply had time to die? Had he sent his strange letter to fool me, to set up an appointment for me with his own death? Panicking, I sketched out an untidy heap of hypotheses, each one weirder than the others. I turned towards Rita: who was this woman?

"Rita, you absolutely have to tell me ... "

"I was crazy to bring you here. But you're one of those creatures time manufactures behind the mirrors. You're a lot like him!"

"Like who?"

"Like Alf!"

"Alf?"

"The angel that's lying there in the sand."

"You mean that ... "

"Alfred was buried here."

"Alfred?"

"Alf was an angel. Understand?"

"Sorry, Rita, but I don't understand a thing."

Tears were running down her cheeks again. I didn't know what to say, I hardly dared to move. I simply waited, my neck strangled by my brace. Tears mustn't be rushed.

After a long moment, Rita got up, lit a cigarette, took three long drags, threw away the butt, examined the statue, copied its pose: left forefinger pointing to the sky, the right one close to the lips, saying "Ssshhh!" Then, slowly, she brought down her left forefinger and moved it towards me. The tip of it was planted in my heart. I wanted to tell her something, but she interrupted me.

"Ssshhh! ... You have to leave me alone now. Alf and I have a lot of things to say to one another."

"But Rita ... "

"Ssshhh! ... I'll explain. Not here. Not now. Tonight, on the cliff, in the temple ruins. Meet me there around midnight. Promise? You'll come? Cross your heart?"

I nodded. Rita smiled, helped me stand up. Before walking through the cemetery gate, I turned around. Rita was bowed over the angel's head. She seemed old. Frail. A butterfly caught on the grey branches of a tree. She was getting ready to bid farewell to life. I walked along the cemetery wall in the direction of the sea. On the beach I found a shelter made of palm fronds, held up by four posts. I went inside the little square of shade that it carved out of the sand's pitiless whiteness. I'd been cast adrift by the sun and the shade was my raft. I questioned the sea before me: "Why did Rita ask me to meet her in the middle of those ruins? Who is buried next to that statue of an angel? Who is the real Alfred Leiris?" The sea gave me no answer. Tiny crabs, stunned by the light, were running around me, burrowing into the sand.

8

Eagle Cliff

I SPENT THE REST OF THE DAY IN ANGUISH. I guzzled beer after beer in the little courtyard of the Hotel Rosario. I was talking to the parrot. I'd felt a growing affection for him. I was afraid that men in uniform were going to come and arrest me. I hadn't had the guts to explain my accident to the rental agency and advise them that the bike was a total loss. I was torn between a desire to leave, to disappear as soon as I could, to wipe out any sign of my arrival on Mexican soil and a desire to be with Rita again. I went over the events of the past few days. I couldn't help imagining some machination of which I was the victim. Together, Alfred, Rita, and the inhabitants of Isla Mujeres formed a dark mass that had come together to surround me on all sides. I shot up like a bullet, stared at the parrot's pinhead eye, then sat down again, declaring myself paranoid.

With nightfall, I calmed down a little. A hint of cool air wiped away my sweat and my doubts. I ordered an omelette, as bare as possible. I ate it hunched in the shadows of my room. I looked at my watch. Another five hours till the rendezvous. Finally, I decided to pack my bags and leave at dawn, making myself as small as possible. If I could change my plane ticket in Cancún, I'd be back in Montreal in two days. In my agitated brain,

Montreal merged with Anna. Boarding the plane home meant landing directly in her arms. I had forgotten that I'd come to Mexico to get away from the agony of her refusals. I was ready to believe that she'd be at the airport, her arms full of flowers, eyes filled with regrets. Three minutes later I'd packed my bags; I stretched out on the bed, staring at a fly on the ceiling. "And what if I'm handicapped now?" I raced to the bathroom. Stood at the mirror above the sink. "Maybe I don't have a neck any more?" I stretched out on the bed again. I hadn't dared to take off my neck brace. I tried to locate the fly on the ceiling. It wasn't there. The fly, not me, had flown away.

When I woke up, I weighed a ton. And I had no idea where that ton of amazement came from. It was dark. I rolled onto the floor. A tiny phosphorescent spot was moving before my eyes. I watched its jerky movements, which traced a circle. A watch! It was my watch, the hands showed 11:00 P.M. The rendezvous. I sprang to my feet. I was going to see Rita again.

A few seconds later I was on the street, running towards the wharf. I found a taxi, stammered delirious explanations to the drowsy driver, and he started his car.

Settled comfortably in the back seat, I was smiling. Light, light as the parrot's green feather! I'd found again the lightness in the wind that was blowing in the open window. A wind that had broken away from the night and the sea, having stolen its most subtle scents. I was worth no more than a dog in a car, but the beauty of the world had spread the word and now appeared to me in all the power of its simplicity. The moon! Never had I seen a moon as swollen, as impudent as the moon that night. Depending on what twists and turns the car took, she appeared unexpectedly, plunging me into wonder. How could she be so round, so carnal, so milky when in

Montreal she was no bigger than a dime? And the chalky light that she spread! The earth was glittering, the sea burning in peaceful ecstasy. The leaves were swaying on the trees, changing from blue to green. The heads of the palm trees, scattered like savage streetlamps, were bathed in a purple halo. Globes! I trembled.

I looked at the nape of the driver's dark neck. This unknown person had been given a mission. He was taking me to the heart of a mystery. With his hands on the wheel, he was assuming responsibility for my destiny. I no longer belonged to myself. I refused to go beyond what I could see. I questioned nothing. The taxi stopped. The driver turned his head, looked at me, waited. I didn't move a muscle. He shrugged as if to say, "Well?" I glanced outside: we'd stopped at a junction. The driver got out of the car. Waved his arm, repeating: "*¿Por aquí o por acá?*" This way or that way? I had no idea. How could I recall the road we'd taken the day before to get to the temple? I'd done it in daylight, haphazardly, intoxicated by the speed of the motorbike. I didn't recognize a thing.

"Me, I, *yo* want to go to *templo* way up there, on the *falaisa*, you *comprendo*?"

"*El hotel Mariposa está aquí, el hotel Merida está acá. Dígame, Señor, ¿dónde quiere ir usted?*"

Obviously, the chauffeur hadn't grasped my intentions at the outset. I tried several versions of the word *temple*: *templa, templo, templaya, tenplayos, templar, templaras*, combined with the same number of *falaisias, falaiyo*, or *falaisianos*, but my Spanish set off no reaction. After several minutes of this experimental linguistic exchange, it seemed obvious to me that the taxi-driver couldn't imagine that, at this hour of the night, a tourist might want any destination but his hotel. I looked at my watch: 11:25 P.M. I took a deep breath and launched into a frantic nonverbal improvisation. Wanting to imitate the scattering of the ruins, I hopped up and down, waving my arms, hoping that my observer would see in my movements the tremors of time, as relentless as a pneumatic drill, demolishing the dense stones of a temple. I only managed to plunge the taxi-driver into sorrow. His face took on the features of a dog sympathizing with the distress of the human race. He probably thought I'd just suffered an epileptic seizure or a bout of tropical fever. He pointed to my neck brace, repeating: "*¡Pobrecito! ¡Tiene muchos problemas usted!*" Defeated, I dropped my arms. Soon it would be midnight. Time to be inventive, if not brilliant. I recalled the guide's explanations about the cliff, its meaning, its use. I switched to another scenario. I grabbed an imaginary knife, drove it into my chest, and pulled it out, a quivering heart at its tip. Then, using the back of my hand to draw the steps of a staircase, I made a little fellow climb up it, then immediately made him tumble down. Hands joined above my head, I imitated a plunge to his death that reached its finale with a loud splash. I concluded with an undulating movement of my hands that faded into a silent, invisible line. The victim flung from the cliff had been swallowed up by the waves of the sea. The taxi-driver slapped his forehead.

"*¡Entiendo, entiendo muy bien!*"

With a victorious gesture, the driver pointed to the side road on the left. I got back in the car with exclamations of *pronto, pronto*. A few minutes later the driver braked in front of an imposing wrought-iron gate lined with bushes pruned into the shape of a lion cub. Where were we? The driver had got out of the car and was yelling "*¡hola! hola!*" I tried to stop him. I was rather agitated and was starting to think that making a rendezvous with one's own fate took a lot of organization. The driver was yelling louder. I clutched him, dragged him back to the car and tried to make him start it. He insisted on going back to the gate and calling I don't know whom. A voice in the distance replied. The driver turned to me with a satisfied smile. He started to wave his arms, spatter the air, to shake himself like a wet dog. I could see that he was imitating my own imitation, but I didn't get what he was getting at. A man came up to the gate. There was a discussion. He opened the gate. The driver pulled me in after him. Made me follow a gravel path lit by lanterns nestled in some exotic bushes. And with no warning, at a bend in a row of giant cactuses, he pushed me to a horseshoe-shaped swimming pool. Proud of himself, the driver pointed to a diving board at least ten metres high, an enigmatic totem gleaming there, unnoticed. What had he imagined? That in the middle of the night, stricken by an irresistible urge to execute some spins and jack-knife dives, I'd gone off in search of the diving-board of a lifetime?

"*Señor, el hotel Mariposa tiene una alberca divina. ¡Mira, mira, es una maravilla!*"

"No, *no*, not hotel, not *piscina, yo* want … "

Why argue with him? I set off towards the little path lined with lanterns, but instead of taking me back to the wrought-iron gate, it led to a tennis court surrounded by tables and parasols and, in the background, the majestic façade of a hotel. In front, strung up on a vaulted portal, neon letters spelled out: MARIPOSA. I was lost. I retraced my steps with the greatest care, looking warily at every square metre of space that I crossed. I was relieved to see the pool. Neither the taxi-driver nor the man who had opened the gate was there. I leaned over the water and scanned the bottom of the pool as if it were the perfect place for a taxi-driver to wait for his fare. I saw my own reflection and the moon's. Two circles. I couldn't help myself, I used that moment to speak to the four-lettered ghost: "I'm a dog, I am trembling because I don't know anything, every step I take adds to the lie that I haul around on this earth, why did I come to Mexico, Anna moon, I hear you laughing under the water, why wasn't I content with photographing whales in the Saguenay ... " Squealing tires broke into my ramblings. The taxi! I ran. Not knowing where I was going, I came to the front gate. I spotted the taxi which was driving away. I was out of breath. I shouted: "*¡Hola!* Taxi! Taxi! *¡stoppo!*" The taxi stopped. I crawled to it, dived inside. The driver started up, calling to me:

"*¿Qué pasó? ¿Dónde estuviste?*"

He thought that I'd snuck away without paying. He wasn't very happy. As for me, I was showing signs of impatience. Midnight was approaching and I had the impression that the driver was heading for another hotel with pool and tennis court, and that after it, there would be another and another ... The prospect of spending the night bouncing from place to place like a billiard ball made the blood rise to my head. I started to howl. The driver stopped. I took out a wad of pesos and threw them at his face, then I ejected myself from the taxi as if I were being pursued by fire. Without picking up the money, the driver sped away, shouting words that got through without subtitles. I was alone. Alone in the Mexican night with my big deep-sea diver's head on my crippled shoulders.

I peered at the overly calm sky. Sat down in the middle of the road. Twenty minutes to midnight. I ran my palms over the warm, soft asphalt. It made me want to lie down, to forget, and wait until tires ran over me. Not now. Rita was waiting for me, probably nearby.

Determined, intrepid, I got up and walked off the road. Confident in my body's compass, I plunged bravely into the bushes. Very soon I stumbled on a clump of roots and flopped full-length, face to the ground. Pulling myself up, I hit my head on a branch. I fell again, this time on my back. A little yellow light wavered, weakened, went out. I was dead.

I used that time to dream. Anna sail, I dreamed a dream that you'd already dreamed. Like you, I was on a ship. It shrank. Then I was on a tiny raft that the waves were playfully lifting up. Like you, to keep from seeing the waves I lay on my back and looked up at the sun. Like you, I began to disappear. To dissolve until the moment when a butterfly settled on my nose. I woke up. There was indeed a butterfly on my nose. I fluttered my eyelids. It flew away.

I looked at my watch. The glass had shattered when I fell, but the second hand was still moving: one minute to midnight. I would be late for my rendezvous with Rita. I wasted the last minute watching the minute hand completely cover the hour hand: midnight. That's it. Now what? I turned towards the moon. I spoke to her white eye: "I have the soul of a stray dog. Though I howl and lament, your impassive halo does not shiver. Moon over Isla Mujeres, take my photo and send the negative to Anna. Let her know that a stray dog in the Caribbean, with your reflection deep in her eyes, is thinking about her!"

Before I'd completed my wish, the moon became creased like tissue paper. Tore herself into pieces that fluttered in every direction: a cloud of butterflies had just swept across the sky. The swarm formed a flash of colour in the night, spread like a powder trail. I ran after it. I tumbled down a path, skirted a pile of rocks that concealed an inlet. Now I was on a beach, an enclave of mauve sand that glittered in the moonlight. I saw the butterflies disappear behind a rock. Their phosphorescent wings had traced a path of light in the sky.

I got undressed, made a bundle of my clothes, and tied it around my waist. I advanced into the sea, in search of butterflies. The moon was doing its job so well that I could make out some tiny fish with blue and lemon streaks. I was swimming now like a frog, now like a dog, because of my neck brace. I was able to go beyond the tip of the inlet. I sat down in the water to catch my breath and inspect the premises: no butterflies, but another inlet. Would I have to begin all over? I got up. I fell and landed back in the water. I'd just caught sight of a long, dark shape parked under the water, barely covered by the waves that passed over it without making an impression. A big fish? Not a shark—I couldn't see a fin. The thing did not respond. I took a step in its direction. Then another. I recognized Adamo, my bike. I'd found the cliff! Immediately, I looked up. Rita must be waiting for me up there, in the ruins of the temple.

I got out of the water. Wrung out my clothes, my pesos, my running shoes. How was I going to climb up there? Eagle Cliff: its name came back to my lips. I tried to distinguish in the rocky mass the proud bearing of a bird of prey or the span of its deployed wings. Nothing. Only rock. I called to Rita. Shouted her name several times in the hope that up there, her head would appear. No one. Then I stood sideways. That way, my voice might have a better chance of carrying. I cried out again. No Rita. An eagle, though. I could make out its profile: the head, the eye, the hooked beak. I just had to change the angle I was looking from and that apparition was cancelled out by the natural muddle of the cliff. Hadn't the guide said that it formed a natural staircase which was an extension of the temple's? With water trickling from my boxers, I set off to conquer the eagle.

After I'd climbed up its claws, I came to a road made of fallen rocks and fissures, of peaks and faults. I climbed higher. I had goosebumps. A powerful breeze coming from sea currents was blowing. Higher up, I spotted a bulge that soared into space: the eagle's beak. That meant I must be at the level of its chest. A sudden burst of love swept through me. Of myself. The thought that an unsteady movement of a hand or foot would cause me to share Adamo's fate made me precious in my own eyes. My fingers were bleeding, my scratched legs were shaking, I climbed, I climbed. Pain transformed my will into determination. Breathless, I arrived at the rocky springboard of the beak. I could climb no higher. My ascent had brought me to the entrance to a cave: the eye.

I had no choice. It was either come down or go in. I ventured a step into the cave. Immediately, I experienced an olfactory hallucination. As if a flower had sprung up to my nose. I went deeper inside, testing the ground with the tips of my toes, fearing a trap or a hole that would swallow me on the spot. The scent persisted. I imagined a fleshy flower that had collapsed under its own heavy petals. The darkness deepened, I disappeared. I coughed hypocritically to check whether anyone could hear me. The lunar brightness that had wavered all around the cave had dispersed. I was at the heart of the darkness. I had sunk into a funnel of stone. I took a few more steps, my body brushing against the rock. Banged into something. The end.

Without trying to, I'd found the end of the world. And suffocation. I realized it now: I didn't have enough air. I wanted to get out. Impossible. Had the walls closed in on me? I turned around several times before I found the passage that put me on the way to the exit. I calmed down. Another whiff of perfume. No doubt about it, that fragrance was coming from the back of the grotto. I had no idea what this was all about. A hallucination? My nose kept saying no. The perfume really was coming from something or someone. Had I actually gone to the very back of the cave? It seemed to me that I had. I resumed walking towards the exit. That was when I recognized the perfume: Rita had worn it at our *huachinango* meal. Smelling it in the dark had made the aroma ten times as potent, had weighed down the vapours. No doubt about it, it was Rita's perfume.

With my nose on the alert, I retraced my steps and plunged again into the gulf of the grotto. Very carefully, I tried to find a fault I might not have noticed. Finally I came up against the same dead end. I concentrated on the perfume. It came in irregular waves, stagnated, evaporated, then poured out again. Why hadn't I realized it sooner? I looked up. A faint, barely perceptible glimmer was thinning the darkness above my head. The perfume wasn't rising, it was descending! I reached up: my hands discovered an opening. I hoisted myself onto the tips of my toes and managed to stick my head inside. By pushing with my feet, I was able to edge my way laboriously into the narrow opening, climbing towards that pale sheet of light six metres higher. Exhausted, I stuck my head out of the darkness and the rock. There I was face to face with myself. My own face was looking at me. The angel of the Isla Mujeres cemetery!

9

The Sacrifice

I EXTRICATED MYSELF FROM THE OPENING. I had just entered a vast, rounded, finely-worked cave, its floor levelled. From the angel head in the middle came a gentle presence. Who had brought it here to the heart of the cliff? Rita. Who else? It sat on the ground, bathed in the light from several candles and animated by the wavering shadows. I felt as if I were at a friend's house in his absence. I knelt. Alf, Alfred? The angel seemed unwilling to reply. His right forefinger was still pressed against his lips and more than ever he was saying, "Ssshhh!"

I called out to Rita. The echo of my voice was the only response. Her perfume though was prowling like a ghost. I picked up a candle and got to my feet. I explored the premises. I must have been in the part that corresponded to the eagle's brain. This grotto was its skull. I kept an eye on the candle flame. It was still tilting in the same direction. I realized that I was in a draft. I turned to go in the opposite direction. The grotto, which I'd thought was round, stretched out and shrank into a corridor that curved slightly inwards. I walked down it and at the end, I spotted a ray of light that fell directly onto a staircase carved into the stone: the exit. I ran and climbed up the steps as if they were taking me to the heart of the truth. I thought about what Alfred Leiris had said: "A flower, you understand, a flower that grows ineluctably. Fate." The moon appeared. I stepped into the bright night. I had just emerged from the temple ruins, in the very spot where only the day before, I'd seen Rita appear, wearing a straw hat. Down below, I recognized the site of the Eagle Stone and the remnants of the staircase that descended to the cliff. I spotted a white shape floating on the farthest point of the rock. Two great wings seemed about to soar into space. Rita was committing suicide before my eyes! I hurtled down the stones, ran, ran, arms held out before me as if they could stretch out infinitely and take hold of her in space!

"Wait! Here I am! Look, I've come to our rendezvous! Rita!"

I thought about her despair, about the illness that was eating away at her. About the fabulous words that only she had the gift to pronounce. I cried out those other words that I hoped would be transformed into a safety net.

"I love you!"

"You're late."

She had turned around, looking away from the abyss. I caught her and held her tight.

"You're shaking, Huachi!"

"I was so afraid you were … "

"You thought that I was going to … but don't rush things, and even more, don't confuse them."

Her perfume, cruel, was making me dizzy. She had taken my hand. She was floating in her diaphanous robe with its flared sleeves. There were thousands of things that I wanted to say to her, and make her say them too; I was silent. Her presence clouded my thinking.

"You're a virgin, aren't you?"

Time stopped. The blood deserted my heart. I turned red. How could she say that? Was it written on my face? Had I been that clumsy on the cemetery sand? One word came from my lips, the tiniest I could think of:

"Yes."

I could make out her body under the light veil of her robe. Rita unfolded her wings and spoke to the vastness of the night.

"My body can no longer recognize joy or sorrow. It's become a sigh. But tonight, tonight … ah … come, come!"

She swept me along with her. I thought to myself: "That's it, we're off. I'm a Mexican dog, a sublime beast, my howl will be heard all the way to Montreal, Anna won't get any sleep tonight." Near the ruins that concealed the entrance to the grotto, Rita bent down to pick up something. A canvas bag. From it she took a flashlight. Switched it on and thrust its beam deep into the stony ground as if she had the power to open it partway.

"Don't be afraid. Don't speak even if I ask you questions. Has anyone ever told you that you have thighs?"

"No."

"Ssshhh! Your thighs aren't well-developed, but they're adorable. Slightly muscular, but slim. No fat. Nothing sagging. Tapered. Two columns. Do you realize what recklessness your thighs give off?"

"No."

"Ssshhh! Remember now. Be silent."

I concentrated on the circle of light that brought the steps of the staircase into view beneath our footsteps.

"Do you realize that your thighs radiate? That they launch appeals? That I receive them? Your thighs are female dogs. Vigilant guardians. I understand them."

Was it her very imminent death that made her so dazzling?

"You will do as I ask. Here, we've arrived. Impressed? Have you any idea where we are?"

This time I said nothing.

"We're at the heart of the world. *Heart.* A word that's become meaningless. Except here."

She directed the light from the flashlight at the angel's head. The stone face was set ablaze. Rita switched it off, thrusting her head back into the wavering light from the candles scattered all around. Our shadows were dancing on the rock walls.

"Sit down, don't move."

I sat cross-legged on the ground. Rita approached me. Let out a long exhalation. She'd eaten garlic. That smell usually makes me recoil, but not now. On the contrary, I leaned forward to bathe in the aroma some more, which speeded up the beating of my heart.

"Close your eyes."

Her voice had the power to transform me into docile matter. My eyelids melted onto my cheeks. Delicately, Rita pressed the palms of her hands on my face. The heat from her body passed into mine. Her fingers searched the arch of my eyebrows, glided onto the bridge of my nose, rested on the timid beginning of a dimple on my chin.

"You can open your eyes if you want."

I opened them. She was rummaging in her bag. Extricated a round package. Untied it. It was a lump of clay, wrapped in a wet cloth that could have been a thin cotton towel. I was shaken by a number of questions. But I didn't open my mouth. Being mute added to my excitement. Part of my being, the most ancient part, had made the decision to obey that woman's every wish.

"I feel like a tango. A music that is obstinate and melancholy. Have you ever been bitten by melancholy? Suffering combined with pleasure! Death by tango—wouldn't that be a dignified way to go? But there's no more tango. Does anyone complain? No one wants to tango any more. We're all alone in the world, Huachitango."

Rita had started crooning softly. She arranged the candles in a semi-circle around me, removing the angel's halo. She put on huge, red-framed glasses and started to knead the lump of clay. She'd set it on a heap of stones that in the dimness looked somewhat like a thickset body. Little by little, she made features emerge from beneath her fingers. Now and then she would approach me, capture a detail, then go back and print it on my clay double. Happiness took hold of me. Happiness that was calm, proud, that gave my pose a solid foundation. "Don't rush, take your time, I understand you perfectly." That was what I told myself behind the mask I was composing for the circumstances. It was clear that Rita loved me. With a venomous love. Wasn't I an expert in the field? Wasn't I an exemplary patient suffering from the malady of love? How many days and nights had I struggled along in a coma, kept alive artificially thanks to my stock of Anna which I was developing, parsimoniously, in my darkroom? By moulding this head in my image, Rita was obeying the same laws that had driven me to store up, over a period of more than ten painful years, the snapshots of my obsession.

"You have the thighs of a tango dancer. Nervous. Aggressive. With your Greek profile you'll take some doing. Beauty can only be a vulgar pile, a hybrid package, a stack."

Rita stroked the clay, smoothed it, made it gleam.

"And that's what I like about beauty: its powerful vulgarity that puts people at ease. You are at ease now, aren't you? I didn't shock you? This grotto, you know, was originally used as a waiting room. A gaggle of sweating thighs would be waiting here. Ah, tango, tango, the elongated shape of the thigh makes you think of a fish. Rubbing a thigh is the only poetic experience still possible nowadays. A thigh swims in space. You dream only of harpooning it. Unearthing top-quality thigh isn't easy. But believing that the essential is found in the thigh is totally naïve. The thigh is a fish, an arrow, a road that leads to the essential. Ah, tango, tango, the thigh sacrifices itself, keeps its prodigious power in the background for the benefit of the ideal. That's why the thigh is the cradle of the divine. It's still the only place where the roar of the origin of the world can be heard. I told you some nonsense about the Aztecs and their human sacrifices. Nonsense. The Aztecs were dwarves. Blind, their eyes clogged with the blood of their victims. They used the sun as a trash can. They got rid of the finest examples of their species because they trembled at the thought of holding them in their arms."

Rita kept working on her mound of clay, talking all the while. Now and then she even gave it a smack, and the dull thud resonated lugubriously in the grotto.

"The acrid sweat of thighs. Just concentrate and you can smell it. How many young warriors could stand here, pressed against one another? A good hundred. Imagine the fidgeting. One Mayan subtlety is worth more than a thousand Aztec brutalities. The historians of the past were wrong, today's are too. Their interpretation of the facts is a joke and so are their attempts to shed light on the past. The only thing all those historians have produced is some grotesque gobbledygook about the customs on this island.

They actually invented a cosmic function for it. A cosmic function, no less! According to those historians, during the glorious era of Isla Mujeres, all the male thighs were part of a cosmic function, dancing to the sound of the fertility drum. And there's the word: fertility. When historians latch onto a term they don't let go of it for a good long time. They're like dogs gnawing at a bone. Where did they get the idea that this island was devoted to a fertility cult, that only virgin boys were sacrificed there—by pulling out you-know-what and then getting rid of them by throwing them off the cliff? How could they stoop to such vulgarity? How could they link fertility with massacre? How could they imagine women being responsible for such a slaughter? Those historians even went so far as to declare that the island was ruled by women, which, from their point of view, was an exceptional situation, worthy to be gone over with the fine-toothed comb of their theory. Unfathomable stupidity and deception. Women would never have behaved like men. But that's not what I want to talk about with you. I want to talk about sex."

Rita had looked up in my direction. She had spoken that last word with fire in her eyes. I shuddered. Was I finally going to experience ecstasy? Limits exist. My virginity was finally going to reach its. And all that power seething inside me was going to ...

"I hear your thighs. They're jubilant. Startled. Your thighs hate historians too. They don't need hypotheses to shudder. They blend naturally into the orchestra of sex. They vibrate. They resonate in harmony with this island, this grotto, their true history. Your thighs know what really happened here. They laugh at hollow concepts, at false interpretations. They're well aware that there were never any women on the Island of Women. That there were only boys. Young men. Gathered in this grotto by the dozen. Merged as they waited. Flattened, muffled, tangled, compressed, brought to the boil. The trance of your thighs undoes the numbness of this cliff, weakens its stone.

"The smell.

"It's there. The smell of sex. It escapes from cracks in the dark. From the porosity of time. It envelops us, reveals us to ourselves. It tells us the unthinkable. Defies us to follow in its consequences. Your thighs are tango. They have nothing more to learn. They are light, memory. They come back to life. They see the raw material of boys kneaded by a desire with no beginning. Material that obliterates the most stubborn angles: elbows, knees, shoulders, hips. They see the beauty of faces faded, erased, confused with hunger. They see the dance without its dancers. Finally, they see sex rid of its worst enemy: the face. They see sex cleave the waters of the mirror, shatter it. The boys are carried away in the wave of sex that unfurls before them, ruffles them, topples them, pumps them. Sex gains all the ground, fills the grotto, enlarges it, swells it, overwhelms it. Sex rages, sex shakes up, sex explodes. There are no more boys. In the grotto, there is an impulse. In the grotto, there is the sound of thighs, an inferno of switchblade thighs bathed in sweat and they decide. The thighs decide. They go out, overcharged, they climb the stone steps, cleave the night with their arrival. Up there, from the ground, there finally emerges sex. Unique muscle. Facing the wind, facing the sea. An immense beast stamping its feet. A brawny torch that makes the dust rise. Tango. Sex is born. Sex licks the sky. Sex laughs, gallops. Sex is alcohol. Sex is a swarm of boys who rise and fling themselves into the void. They throw themselves off the cliff like a single chariot. But instead of falling, they take flight. They rise up. Spasm. Ecstasy. A splatter."

Rita had talked faster and faster. Her narrative had wakened all my senses. I couldn't take any more. I got up, legs shaky, went to her.

"Do you recognize yourself? It's not exactly what I'd intended to do. Inspiration of the moment."

She presented her work to me. Instead of a head, mine, I was gazing at an enormous phallus.

"You can talk now."

I couldn't.

"You've got a funny look on your face! I'm misleading you with all those words I've been spouting. Don't let them impress you. Touch it. Damp clay is very much like human skin. But cold. Sit down. I'm miserable. I've bothered you with my nonsense, my ravings. I can't help it, when I'm nervous I make these unbelievably stupid remarks. I let myself get carried away. Say whatever comes into my head. Anything, absolutely anything that comes into my head. Forget it all."

She took off her glasses, lit a cigarette. Took a long drag. Should I make the first move? I sat down again.

"Look at me. What do you see? Look at my boobs. Look at my hips. What did you really see? A face, breasts, hips. Look at my face again. Look closely at the skin of my cheeks, my chin. I'll come closer to the candles. Take a good look at my skin. Do you understand? No? You're a virgin. I knew that your Greek profile would be a sign of great purity. I am ugly. I'm also old. Older than you think. I have no breasts. You can see for yourself. You already have, in any case. This skin of mine. I'd do without it if I could. Who can live without? You're surprised, I can see, you've been flirting with old skin. We're comfortable here in this grotto. Even if the heat is draining us. We can sense that it's letting go. We won't be able to hold in anything, you and I. That will be good. Alf didn't have a Greek profile as pure as yours. He was made of something crumbly. Any boy who's too handsome is dangerous. Especially to himself."

Rita had approached me. I got up to take her. Now was the moment. My whole body was telling me that. But Rita pulled back abruptly, grabbed her hair, pulled it. Then presented to me, like a trophy, the wig that she held in her hand.

"So, Christophe, you haven't gone to Belize?"

"Alfred Leiris!"

I recoiled as if I'd just been bitten by a snake.

"Don't be frightened. Dancing shadows, that's all we are."

"But who are you?"

"A man, Christophe. Like you."

"I don't understand."

"There's no face between us any more."

"That doesn't make any sense. You can't be a man."

"You're right. I can't be a man. Neither can you. Who can be a man, who? The two of us? We are nothing. Let's enjoy it. Fate. The little flower of fate, inane and sickly sweet, that you've stuck between your teeth. Let's laugh, Christophe, let's laugh at the ancient sacrifices. Let us think of those that are coming now."

"Who are you?"

"My name is Pierre Tourelle."

I looked at her in disbelief. The dim light in the grotto made her enigmatic. She opened her bag. I thought she was going to show me her passport to prove her identity. But she produced a piece of yellowed paper. She unfolded it and gave it to me to read.

"I've never been able to throw this away."

It was a newspaper clipping. Intrigued, I moved closer to the candles.

THE FABULOUS JOURNEY OF THE MONARCHS

Every year the monarchs travel nearly 5000 kilometres. Fleeing the rigours of the Canadian winter, these Lepidoptera reproduce in the Mexican heat. Monarchs seem to be useless. They do not serve as food for other animal species. Their brilliant colour, fluctuating between red and orange, indicates the toxicity of their wings to potential predators. They fly at an average speed of thirty-two kilometres an hour, taking full advantage of the winds. These fragile and gracious butterflies need close to two months to reach the South. Their migration is attracting more and more tourists. The sight of such a storm of colours raining onto the ground, the trees, the roads is unforgettable. Research to date has identified three migratory routes. Monarchs living west of the Rockies go to California. Those that live east of the Rockies and around the Great Lakes go to Michoacán in the Sierra Chincua. Finally, monarchs from the Atlantic provinces cross Carolina and Florida to winter, it is believed, in Cuba and the Yucatán Peninsula. For the latter however the precise destination is still a mystery. It is now known that the monarchs' migratory route brings them to Isla Mujeres—the Island of Women—a tiny land mass in the Yucatán, using it as a rest area for just a few hours, then taking off again for their final destination, which is still unknown. The Atlantic monarchs depart the northern regions much earlier than other species. Only the last generation of monarchs goes on this fascinating journey. Gorging themselves on nectar, they postpone their sexual maturation so they can mate in the South. According to a local legend, the millions of monarchs that swoop down on Isla Mujeres and then quickly depart consist of those individuals of the species that cannot hold back any longer their need (or desire!) to mate. The past of this island, famous for its fertility rituals, has no doubt contributed to this belief.

Lorrina Calvinot

"So? I don't get it. Why did you want me to read that?"

Rita took the clipping, folded it carefully, put it back in her bag.

"The butterflies."

"The butterflies what?"

"I knew someone who thought they were the most sacred creatures in the universe. That person couldn't stand to see them pinned down under glass. Her name was Bianca. She felt every stab of the needle in her heart. She used to say that when they were dead, those insects didn't rot. In her opinion, humans were an inferior species, filled with revolting, putrid matter. She also told me that the muscles which activate a butterfly's wings are the exemplary muscles of love: hidden, small, powerful. Do you know why? Because the extreme fragility of a creature is moving. Do you understand?"

"I'm not sure I do."

"A butterfly. Bianca was a butterfly. Meeting her was a shock to me. She stole the air around her. The only way to avoid asphyxiation was to live as close as possible to her mouth. In the beginning, I behaved like a genuine knight with her. I walked ahead so I could open the door for her,

I covered her with flowers, kissed her fingertips. She dropped a half-hearted kiss on my cheek, said once again that we would have to wait. It was driving me crazy. One day, I couldn't help it, I jumped her. She struggled, delivered three or four punches. I thought it was over with us. But instead of showering me with insults, Bianca gave me the clipping you've just read. Then she said, 'Imagine the anguish of a larva, a little blob of grease hesitating between life and death. One part decomposes and another, like a vulture, eats it. It's a battle between formlessness and fervour. On the day when fervour prevails over formlessness, the butterfly rips open its cocoon. That day is the night. The night of love.' Bianca gave off the fragrance a child, of raspberries. She told me, 'Pierre, take me to the Island of Women.' Her remark cut through her tears like a knife. We left for Mexico. We arrived at Isla Mujeres. On the subject of the monarchs, Bianca had often told me, 'A watch tick-tocks in their genes and programs them.' She liked the inescapable, complained about the unpredictable nature of man. I retorted that I preferred the uncomfortable freedom of man to the booby-trapped fate of the butterfly, which is constrained to immolate itself in the flame of a candle. My arguments had no effect on her passion—or I should say her obsession. Twenty years ago, on this very cliff, we watched for the monarchs' programmed arrival. When the muffled hum of the swarm became perceptible, Bianca said to me, 'This is the most beautiful moment of my life.' The air was vibrating, was warming up. A purple cloud was heading our way. Bianca waved her hands as if the monarchs were sensitive to her signals. The air suffered a spasm. Time began to crackle. The spot of colour stormed the entire sky. Then, all at once, the monarchs pelted down onto the cliff. We were breathing them, swallowing them. They metamorphosed us into bursts of red and orange. Bianca sang, danced, kissed me. I copied her. Myriads of butterflies touched down on the ground and turned it into a downy substance on which we floated in a state of weightlessness. Safe in our suit of ecstasy, Bianca and I blazed like bonfires of torches. We burst out laughing as the blue of the night edged into purple. We were swimming in love that had come from the sky, that had kidnapped the air. Through the curtain of beating wings, I caught sight of Bianca taking off her clothes. Immediately she donned a robe of butterflies. And what a robe it was! Ah, Bianca, Bianca!"

What was Rita getting at with this story?

"Bianca lay down on the ground: a sarcophagus studded with rubies and gold, and I knelt beside it. To gain access to her lips I took away the monarchs gathering nectar from her face. I felt as if I were restoring a work of art. I pressed my lips against hers. Bianca let herself go. Her body lost the magnificent rigidity that had imprisoned her and forbade me to desecrate it. A raging river loosed its torrents in my limbs. Nothing could have held me back. I ate Bianca's mouth, I ate the space of Bianca's mouth, I sucked her tongue, her lips, the flesh of her cheeks, I ploughed her palate with my tongue, which had become harder than a granite battering ram, I swallowed her saliva, wrenched myself away from her mouth so I could bite her chin; I licked her neck, I dug furrows all the way to her breasts, thin, quivering twin fruit so close together that my mouth, unable to choose, tried to swallow their erect tips simultaneously, I wreaked havoc on her nipples; laid waste to them with a gardener's hands, inhaled them, Bianca cried out in pain, ordered me to go on, I went on, I cleared a path for myself all the way to her belly, my mouth foaming with butterflies that my teeth tore to shreds, I was advancing into the life that was throbbing there, creating a clearing, my face smeared with colour and sweat, a tiger was my face, I sucked her navel, the blade of my tongue tried to pierce it, a drum took over my loins, its music shook the ground, with one thrust of my knee I spread Bianca's legs, I slipped my mouth down lower, a branch rose up, covered with butterflies, I blew on them, the sex of a man appeared."

Rita offered me her eyes to gaze at. I was afraid of getting lost in them.

"My Bianca had between her legs a penis, just like me. I tried to bite it off. What! Had I loved a lie? Who was this man? And what about me, who was I to have accepted her whims, to have found them exciting, romantic? I'd waited for two years, reined in my passion. Who but the most sincere lover would have agreed to such a sacrifice? To witness the butterflies' amorous prelude in order to live one's own! To come to the Island of Women and discover that your beloved is a man! What had that man been thinking? That my love would be completely taken in! That the Night of the Butterflies would wipe out any difference! That the Night of the Butterflies would stop me from seeing a man's sex even when there was one! That love, when famished, will eat anything! That the nature of the sex is basically, very basically, merely a detail! I jumped up. I hated that man, that stranger lying at my feet. I couldn't speak. To say what? I left him to his ecstasy. I went away without turning around. I cursed the butterflies that were all around us. Crushing them was a pleasure. I was suffocating. I was furious with the universe, with myself more than anyone else. I heard his voice behind me: 'Don't leave me, Pierre, don't leave me … ' I ran as if getting away from him would cancel out what I'd just experienced. Then I collapsed, crying like a child. I still loved him. I still loved his skin, his smell, his gaze, his smile. What had I done? He had offered me the truth of his being, I'd rejected it brutally. His strength came from not displaying his suffering like a piece of merchandise. I got up again. Turned towards him. My race lasted only as long as an impulse. I stopped short. What was I doing now? I was running, arms held out towards … a man! How could I forget that simple truth? What would I do? Was I the one who'd been unwilling to recognize his true nature? Was it me who was the liar? Was it my eyes that were blind? My heart that was deceitful? Had I also loved the part of her that was a man? These questions paralyzed me. This man, this boy, was goddess, god, beast, larva—a monarch. His wings held sway over my heart. I started running back to him. I was filled with a pure joy. No more questions, no more doubt would well up in me. I spied him in the distance. Just as I was about to call out to him, the millions of Isla Mujeres's butterflies tore themselves from the ground. With a huge commotion they re-formed the cloud in which they'd touched down. I now could see only red. I was at the heart of a storm. The air was torn to shreds. I struggled. The world was coming undone around me and I was coming undone with it. When the tail of the swarm finally left the cliff, the curtain was descending. Too late. This wasn't the beginning of the play, it was the end. A tragic routine. Of lethal beauty. An apotheosis.

Rita bent over. I thought she was feeling faint. But she picked up her wig and fitted it onto her head.

"A splatter, Huachi. Bianca jumped off the cliff. I saw her take flight, holding onto the long robe of monarchs. But it was Alf's body that was smashed against the rocks."

"Alfred!"

"Yes, his name was Alfred, Alfred Leiris."

"I'm sorry."

"Don't be ridiculous."

"But I was … "

"Let me speak, Christophe! A year ago I learned that my days were numbered. I felt no anguish. In fact, new desires arose. One day, to my amazement, I bought a dress. The following days, I struggled with all my power of reasoning, with all my concern for decorum, but it was no good. Defeated, I put it on again. The dress was more powerful than the man I was. The rest—makeup, wig, stiletto heels—followed soon after. I wasn't even able to be surprised. I thought to myself: 'How many days do I have left to live? Enough to be saved.' But from what, since I was going to die? I didn't know. A month ago, when I arrived in Mexico, I thought I'd come on one last pilgrimage. I sculpted that head from a photo of Alfred. It's no coincidence that you should have landed on it yesterday. I'd just substituted it for the one on his grave. Will you believe me, Christophe, I felt beautiful here. Ridiculous, isn't it? On this island I've realized that vanity is a form of intelligence. A body that transforms itself is a miraculous event. And when it happens without the will of the person who sees himself being transformed, it produces a surprising spectacle. Look at my legs. Admit that there's something about them. Removing the hair from them demands a blind faith. Yes, on this island I've felt a secret garden yearning for the light. Every day for a month, at three o'clock, I visited Alfred's grave as the widow. Every day, more and more precisely, I relived the Night of the Butterflies. And every day, when I left the cemetery, my transformation became more apparent. What giddiness to disappear into another body that is nevertheless your own! What a trick to play on death as it works on you! But let's get to the point: you!"

Rita came towards me, forcing me to flatten myself against the rocky wall of the grotto.

"You! The tick-tock, tick-tock that your presence sets off, tick-tock that has accompanied my heartbeats ever since I caught sight of you on the beach. Do you remember the slap I gave you? My ring cut you. When I saw blood on your lips, I was revolted. But that revulsion was transformed into an uncontrollable desire to bite you. Your presence, your attentiveness, your gaze: something fragile, something tender, something about you that is offered made me want to eat you up."

Rita's breath was crushed against my face. I had to breathe her garlic-laden breath.

"You have the same Greek nose as my dead Alf. The same low forehead. When I saw you with your drawing of me, I wanted to jump you. But I was Pierre Tourelle, someone whose existence was dwindling and becoming more and more difficult. I spoke to you at the hotel reception desk. I was shaking, did you notice? No, of course not. You were looking for a woman. Imagine how flustered I was: you were looking for me. I was right there in front of you. And yet there couldn't have been more distance between us. I don't know what detour, what obscure mathematics made me tell you that the person you were looking for was my wife. But once I'd said those words, I couldn't erase them. I'd just got married to myself. You told me you were leaving for Belize. I wanted to hold you back. So I wrote you the letter that I signed Alfred Leiris. I talked about the uncontrollable appetites of my sick body. About its voracious hunger. I asked you to join me on this island. Do you realize what a poetic shock you gave me when you landed head-first on the site of the Eagle Stone, ejected from a motorbike sprung out of nowhere? Only a splatter has that ability. Or an angel. Why do you resemble my vanished Alf? Can't you guess why I made that date with you? I saved your life. You owe me one."

"What do you mean?"

"Can't you subtract? You owe me a life. And I intend to take it."

"Don't be ridiculous. Let's get out of this grotto."

"You're absolutely right. It's time for us to leave this grotto."

From her purse Rita took a revolver and pointed it at me.

"Pick up the flashlight. Move. I'm behind you. Above all, don't try to run away."

So. Now I knew. Rita had set a trap for me. I was her next victim. I never should have left the shore of your face, Anna horizon, even if it meant entangling myself in the barbed wire of your indifference.

"I feel huge, elastic. I am WOMAN. I have six arms, eight mouths, hundreds of teeth. I want to bite the nape of your neck. To lick your hair. Keep moving."

While Rita was raving I thought up plans for escape: feign an epileptic fit, miss a step, land on her, turn around and blind her with the flashlight, or plunge us both into the dark. All these scenarios were risky. Rita would have more than enough time to riddle me with bullets. I tried to reassure myself: "She'd never dare to hurt me, she's too smart, she loves me, I have a Greek profile."

"It's ridiculous, Huachi, but I can't stop myself from telling you what I'm thinking. And I won't ask you to guess, because you wouldn't stand a chance."

Rita came out with a little laugh. I let one out too, nervous and even more curt than hers.

"What I'm thinking is that I'm a shrimp."

"A shrimp?"

Rita's laugh swelled like a wave and washed into the grotto, echoing there.

"I'm a three-year-old shrimp. Did you hear me? A three-year-old shrimp."

"Yes, yes, I heard you."

"I read that a shrimp is male at birth and turns female in its third year. Isn't that hilarious?"

"Yes, hilarious."

Rita was silent until we stepped out of the grotto. The sea breeze welcomed us as two ghostly spirits emerging from the ground. At the risk of my life, I turned around and faced Rita.

"Listen, it's late. I'm falling asleep on my feet. I'm very glad to have known you. You have problems, everyone has problems, that's no reason to ... "

An explosion ripped through the night. I sank to the ground.

"Get up! I fired into the air."

"Don't do it again!"

"Kiss me."

"Do you think that's necessary?"

"Do you want me to shoot you down like a rabbit?"

Like a robot I got up, walked towards Rita. She kissed me, the revolver against my stomach. I thought that kiss would never end. I remembered the nightmare in which I killed a rabbit. Anna, I could feel in my bones that life was insignificant. And feeling it so acutely relieved me.

"Sex. It's not about that. You aren't sexy. You're absolutely ridiculous in your running shoes and shorts and your neck brace. Do you think you're the very image of a lover? That you arouse desire? What do you suppose?

That I'm going to rape you? You look disappointed. Who do you think you are? You're nothing, nothing, nothing! And yet ... innocence clothes you like a skin. I lied to you. Historians make up the most wonderful stories in the world. They grasp the only truth that matters. You and I will know it. You are nothing. But I'm less than nothing. I want you to be the god of my death. I saved your life. Take mine. We'll be even."

"Take your life?"

"In the spot where your feet are now lay, long ago, the Eagle Stone, the sacrificial stone."

Rita rummaged in her purse. I had the impression that she could take out of it whatever she wanted—a piano, a rhinoceros. She no longer bothered to aim at me. Something in the air had changed. The chalky light of the moon seemed to be saying: everything is possible. The night and its appendages—our two silhouettes—were undulating in blue, fairy-tale vapours. Rita fished a book from her purse. I recognized it right away.

"This is what I was reading on the beach when I heard you crying for help."

Everyone is mistaken about the profound meaning of the sacrifice. He who is sacrificed has never been a victim. He has always been one of the chosen. The poem below, attributed to a Mayan cycle from the Island of Women, is proof of that.

> *When the sea has drunk the sun*
> *I shall lie down on the stone*
> *and wet it with tears of joy*
> *for a long time now I've been waiting*
> *my boyish body rejoices*
> *the thirteen years of my life*
> *too many now*

will roll like gold
onto the angry rocks
I shall experience love
on the sharp edge of time
I am the chosen of the island
I am the island of the night.

Rita's eyes filled with tears. She closed them and repeated:

I am the chosen of the island
I am the island of the night.

I could smell her perfume again. How many stars were shining above our heads? An incredible number that were misdirecting us into the present.

"Ah! To be on the edge, to taste, to taste the abyss that opens like a fruit! Alfred brought me to the edge of a chasm. I bless him, I mourn him still. Christophe, you see before you a young woman. I have just barely been born. I am even too young to imagine the things that lovers do. But I'm ready: I shall be the first young girl to be sacrificed on the Island of Women. Huachi, open my heart. Right here. With that."

Rita rummaged in her purse again, took out a towel-wrapped object which she handed me. This time it wasn't a lump of clay. From the towel I took a butcher knife.

"The best way to live is to not fear death. A gown of lace is growing on my body, secreted by my virginity. A sac of poison is about to burst in my nubile body. Despite the tenderness of the night and that of your black eyes, I am rotting. The young girl I am is the Chosen One of this island. A swing which is moving inside me. Calm it. I want to die by your hand. Kill me."

I knelt down. Rita slipped her dress off her shoulders. I had thought that love was the highest peak. But I was now even higher. Down below, time was flowing like a stream. A strange force had just raised me up to the unthinkable: the desire to kill. Anna, my Anna boat, for a moment you departed my heart. A window shut, the memory of you stayed outside. I was new, naked, with a knife in my hand. Rita clutched my head and pulled it up to hers.

"In your eyes now I see only the stars. Hurry! Strike! Can you hear the tango?"

Yes, the chords of a tango were unfurling on the cliff.

"You'll throw my body into the sea. Strike!"

I tore Rita's dress, which was gathered around her loins. All I saw was the body of an old man with spit on his chin.

"Strike!"

Rage extracted a howl from me. I closed my eyes and with all my might, brought down the knife.

"Ahhhhhh!"

"Christophe!"

"Annnnnna!"

10

Strawberry and Kiwi

A NNA STOOD FACING ME. What incredible coincidence had brought her to Eagle Cliff?

"What are you doing here, Anna?"

"Why have you got the kitchen table on your head?"

"What?"

She was right: I had the kitchen table on my head. I laid my burden down. I was gradually emerging from a fog of images and sensations. Mexico, the cliff, Rita, the grotto, the knife—it was all going back to the past whence it had come. How long had I been here under the table, adrift in memories? Anna, in a pale dress, was keeping an eye on me. I started, thunderstruck: Anna is here at my house! The miracle thousands of times hoped for, dreamed of, turned over and over in every direction, had come true. The shock was too brutal. A doubt immediately sprang up: am I not in Mexico, dreaming that I'm dreaming that I'm in Montreal with Anna? Yes: I'm still in Mexico. This Anna is a chimera. A wonderful chimera. I'm dreaming that I'm dreaming that a chimera of Anna in a pale dress, like a spot of moonlight, is looking at me.

"Are you okay, Christophe?"

"I'm fine, how about you? When did you get here?"

"Just now."

"Did you have a good trip?"

"A trip?"

"I'm staying at the Hotel Rosario."

"Are you your normal self?"

"I'm dreaming, Anna."

"You'll never change."

At which point, I fainted.

When I came to, I came back to Anna as well. Who was covering my forehead with cool little kisses. Then I realized unhappily that she was patting my forehead with a damp washcloth.

Yes, I was well and truly in Montreal, in my apartment, with Anna bending over me. No more doubts. I sensed relief in my body: it was weary, empty, but calm. My fever was dropping like a tide that's giving up the ghost on the horizon. I got up to make coffee. Anna was wonderfully silent. I had started to exist for her, in the same room, in the harmony of a soft, slow silence. Sitting across the table from one another, the filter coffee-maker between us, we shared a look and a smile. After a few sips, a conversation emerged from the shell of silence, a little at a time.

Anna told me about her acting career, asked if I'd seen her in the TV series *Cul-de-sac* which she'd starred in, then expressed concern about having found me delirious. I reassured her, explained my misadventure with a jellyfish in the Caribbean Sea. She smiled, nodded, fiddled with a lock of hair, suggested I see a doctor, then changed her mind, reminding me that I wasn't like other people in any event, that she'd seen me in worse shape, that I looked quite well, after all, that she now knew lots of people in the TV world who followed regimens, diets, treatments—and that when all's said and done they still suffered from their usual symptoms and I should thank my lucky stars that I had such a tough body. I thanked her for encouraging me to go on living, thereby bringing out the best in my tortured but tenacious personality. I complimented her on her taste in clothes. She had on a dress so light and luminous, I kept expecting her to take flight. She told me that she'd just signed a very lucrative contract with a jeans manufacturer; that soon I'd be seeing her on billboards, in the metro, on highways, on the brick walls of windowless buildings; that her agent was promising her an international career. I was already imagining the torments I'd live through if I found myself face to face with those giant Annas poured into jeans designed to tame a savage beauty. She turned her head, looked around nonchalantly, let her gaze slip onto the walls of my apartment, which were devoted partly to her, pretending not to notice. For my part, I didn't dare start a laboured explanation of the origin of these photos taken without her knowledge. I got her back on the rails of her career—the better to forget my own, which was pathetic and pitiful. She talked passionately about Isabelle, her character in *Cul-de-sac*, a junkie who lived on the street, a rebellious and adventurous girl who was going to have serious problems with some minor members of the Montreal underworld. I pretended to be delighted, amazed, as if I wanted more, but I couldn't confess to her that when I came back from Mexico, like everyone else I had watched *Cul-de-sac* and stopped after the third episode because I couldn't stand seeing her—even while playing a character, even while reduced to a TV image—in the presence of Lâm, because he too—through what brutal mystery of life?—was in *Cul-de-sac*. And it didn't take a lot of imagination to understand that his character, who went by the name of Tâm, was going to fall under Isabelle's spell, and that the end of the series was going to sanction their union after some highly dangerous adventures, a painful event that I didn't want to bring up; Anna, though, as if she'd just read my mind the better to upset me, insisted on giving me—before anyone else, she insisted—a scoop from the next episode: namely, that Tâm's father was going to be gunned down in his convenience store during a pathetically amateur burglary, that Isabelle would witness it, and that between the young delinquent and Tâm—helpless witness to his father's murder—would be born a love marked by misfortune and fury. She repeated those words: "A love marked by misfortune and fury."

Then, silence. The silence that comes before the announcement of the worst. I wasn't fooled. Anna was there with me in the middle of the night. For that, there was a reason. Since I'd got my lucidity back, I hadn't allowed myself to ask her to explain her surprising visit. How was I supposed to believe that she'd broken into my place, filled with feelings of love? Or that she was deigning at last to respond to the rendezvous I'd made? No, I wasn't taken in.

"Christophe, I'm sure you suspect that I didn't come here in the middle of the night to talk about my acting career."

I started to dream: what if Anna really had come here in the middle of the night filled with feelings of love?

"Have you read the latest *Allô Vedettes*? There's an interview with me where I explain that I've got a very good chance of playing the lead in a big-budget film with an American star. I can't say who, that's a secret. Do you know where I've just come from?"

"No."

"From Toronto. I had been there till only a few hours ago, I went for a second series of auditions. I saw the director, the producers. It went so well that I came back a day early. Are you listening, Christophe?"

"I'm listening, Anna, I'm listening."

"I wanted to give Lâm a surprise, I didn't call to tell him I was coming home tonight. He wasn't expecting me till tomorrow, after all. I took a bath, listened to music, called some friends. No one knew where Lâm was. I figured he was at the movies. There are Friday screenings that end late. Midnight came. No Lâm. I had a kind of premonition. I went through his things. Usually I don't do that sort of thing. I opened the drawer where he keeps his papers. Hidden under a pile of letters, I found a small notebook. Lâm had been keeping a diary. The first entry was a few weeks ago. I started to read it. I was … I was … "

"What did you read?"

"Christophe, if I came to your place in the middle of the night, it was to … "

She didn't complete her remark. The door to my darkroom had just opened. Michèle appeared. Anna froze. Michèle took a step. Anna blanched. She gave me a look of incredulity and disgust. Or was it anger? Before I had time to react, Anna had left. Her footsteps were still echoing on the stairs when Michèle gave a faint, sad smile.

Michèle hadn't left as I had foolishly thought. She was in my darkroom. But for how long? I looked at my watch. Barely twenty minutes had gone by since the moment when, stretched out under the kitchen table, my memories had made me drift all the way to Isla Mujeres. Anna had stayed with me for fifteen minutes. Which cut to five minutes the time I'd taken to relive part of my life. Was it the fever that had speeded up the images of my past till they were reduced to the spasm of a spinning top quickly made immobile again? A slightly faster rotation would perhaps have sufficed for me to disappear from time and—who knows?—from space. I was thinking about that because, as I'd been paralyzed since Anna's departure, part of my person would have preferred to disappear in the face of Michèle's obvious distress. I went to her, held her in my arms. My act didn't convince me. My mind was still with Anna. What had she read in Lâm's notebook? Hadn't she been jealous when she saw Michèle? I existed for Anna. I held Michèle more passionately: Anna loved me. As early as the next day I would speak to her, explain that Michèle didn't matter to me. Reassured by the decision, I was about to bring my embrace to an end when I heard these words: "I want you." Anna was back. I turned towards the door. No one. I returned to Michèle.

"I'm not a deaf-mute. And I'm not what you think either. May I use your phone to call a taxi?"

I pointed to the phone. She walked towards it. She didn't finish punching in the number. Slowly, she took off her sunglasses. Two black eyes appeared, caught between narrow slits. I recognized him: Lâm.

"I'm sorry, Christophe."

"I don't understand ... I'm ... I'm totally ... "

I sat down. Stared at the coffee-maker. Stared at the cup Anna had drunk from. Stared at her lipstick traces on the white rim. Lâm sat down too. Across from me, where Anna had sat. I was mute. A sack of amazement sitting over a cold cup of coffee. After a long moment, Lâm broke the silence.

"I don't know how ... It's very hard for me to ... You know, Christophe, when I was very young I suffered from a strange sensation ... I ... It was as if I were missing a leg or an arm. Not because they'd been torn off in an accident, but because I'd left them behind in a car or on a seat in a

movie theatre. That sensation left me on the day when my
sister, or her spirit, resurfaced in my life. Please, hear me
out. I was living with a foster family at the time, in Saint-
Fulgence; their name was Grenier. They had two children.
Twins: Michel and Micheline. When I arrived in their
house overlooking the Saguenay, I was still traumatized by
my hasty departure from Montreal. My nights were filled
with dread. In the dark, I looked for my parents and
brothers. And my sister, whom I'd seen die. In Montreal
I'd found a remedy for my nocturnal panic. I would slip
into Anna's bed. Do you know what I did in Saint-
Fulgence? The same thing. I would go into Micheline's
bedroom. She adored animals. She imagined that I was a
small animal she'd saved from death. I was her frog. Other
times, her squirrel. Sometimes it was her turn to lick me
with a cat's tongue or pinch me with a goose's beak. Her
imagination provided us with all sorts of appendages—
claws, prying muzzles, velvet paws, wolf's mustaches,
rabbit's ears—which made our pleasure inexhaustible."

Why was Lâm telling me all that?

"One night, sleep forgot about me. It let me toss and
turn in bed to my heart's content. I fell out of bed. My fall
wakened Michel, with whom I shared the room. I told him
I couldn't get to sleep. Michel proposed a solution: the
bear-hug hold. Michel liked to watch wrestling on TV. He
explained that the hold put to sleep anyone unlucky
enough to experience it. It consisted of taking your
opponent from behind and squeezing his ribcage. Which
Michel did to me with all the strength of his arms, the arms
of a child. After a moment I heard him ask: "Are you
asleep?" The poor thing had run out of strength. I was not
asleep. On the contrary, his bear hug had excited me, but
I pretended I'd fallen asleep. He let go of me. I dropped
onto the mattress. Michel repeated his question, with a

victorious intonation: "Are you asleep? Are you really asleep, Lâm?" I began to snore. Michel pressed his head against my heart. Tried to lift me. My phoney sleep weighed a lot. He left me where I was. How I loved the moment when his warm ear touched my heart!

"The next day I couldn't wait to ask him for another bear hug. Michel jumped into my bed, squeezed my chest. But that time, Christophe, I couldn't stay serious. I started laughing uncontrollably. Michel turned me till I was facing him, to make me stop. I laughed even harder. 'What's wrong with you, Lâm? You're out of your mind!' I suddenly had the impression that someone else was laughing inside me. Michel was staring at me. 'If you don't stop laughing I'll call Mama and tell her what you do with my sister when you get into her bed!' His brush-cut hair shot little peaks of defiance into the air. The laughter inside me stopped. 'And what do you think I do with Micheline? I'm sure you have no idea!' Michel performed a headlock, to show me that he had the situation under control. 'Oh yes I do! You play animals.' I broke his hold and scissored him with my legs. 'Did Micheline tell you that?' 'No, I saw it all myself. I spied on you. I'm the biggest spy on earth. Didn't you know?' With no warning, I kissed him on the neck. 'What are you doing?' I started to lick him as if I were a kitten. 'I'm playing animals.' That night, without knowing it, I had offered my dead sister half of my body. It was as if she were laughing inside me. You know, Christophe, I saw some dirty men throw her corpse into the sea. It was on the deck of a ship. I saw my sister disappear into the black waves."

Lâm was silent. I didn't know what to say. He sipped some coffee and went back to his story.

"I soon got into the habit of playing with the twins alternately. One night, Micheline, the next night, Michel.

With him, a shiver sometimes opened my bones the way a knife-tip opens an oyster. I asked him to call me Michèle. I told him I was his second twin. I had two personalities, which doubled my pleasures. And most of all, I no longer felt the need to check and see if I'd lost part of my body when I was running after a dog or coming out of the bath.

"We had a surprise one night when Micheline joined us. Between the twins I savoured all the tastes of harmony joined together. We formed a set of gears whose mechanism, once its cycle was over, wound up again on its own. I was swimming, flying, confusing *above* with *below*. With all our animal sounds, it wasn't long before the Greniers burst into the offenders' room. Once again, I was driven out of my foster family. That time they went to the trouble of explaining why I was being expelled. I learned that I was a monster, a psychopath. Now I had a dossier and the privilege of regular meetings with psychologists.

"After that I spent several years with various families, all of them childless. As soon as I could, I went back to Montreal where I was admitted to the Conservatory of Dramatic Arts. I met Anna by chance on a film set. I was a kiwi in a yoghurt commercial. Anna played a strawberry. When she recognized me, she fainted. In our fruit costumes we laughed and cried. Anna told me that she'd just completed her actor's training at the National Theatre School. I remember that the same evening, we'd gone to see a film at a rep house: *The Exorcist*. Afterwards, the scenes in which the little girl who is possessed spins her head around like a top, spitting obscenities and green snot, still haunted us. Shaking, laughing, we announced that we were the most frightened and the happiest people in the world; breathing in deeply the cool air of the autumn evening; thanking life, passers-by, the streets, the cars, the trees for not being possessed by the forces of evil;

expressing our gratitude to the beauty of the wind-swept city for staying with us as far as Anna's apartment, which I didn't leave until several days later, after the greatest marathon of love I'd ever lived.

"Finally I moved in with her. I was fulfilled, Anna was fulfilled, our careers were taking off faster than we'd imagined. Shortly afterwards you burst into my life. I imagine you remember what burst I'm referring to. In a fraction of a second a gesticulating, howling man was in the middle of our living room which was strewn with broken glass. A man dressed in black, with a kind of hood over his face. Fear of arrest and massacres, something I'd lived through in Vietnam, resurfaced. Fear that was intact, folded over and over and hidden carefully deep inside me. At the time, I thought that the war, like an indefatigable dog, had tracked me down and was about to smother me in its mud. But the war exited the way it had entered—through the window.

"Once I was over the shock, Anna explained that she had finally recognized the madman who'd just jumped from the third floor, taking her coat with him! That was when I heard your name for the first time. Anna thought of you as a friend, a brother. It was for her that you remained a virgin. I couldn't believe such a thing—I who made love several times a week! And how could Anna have lived with someone who took the food scraps from her plate and then savoured them in secret with tears in his eyes? She kicked you out. She thought it was the only solution.

"Months passed. A vapour, a small blue mist had been lurking in my thoughts since I'd known of your existence. I couldn't account for the attraction I felt at the mere notion of your existence. I didn't care about giving words to the sensations that inhabited me for fear that once they were named, they'd have an official value and become fully legitimate. But Michèle is obstinate: she was able to impose her desires. Do you know what I did, Christophe? I re-transcribed your messages. Your *annalexicon*: that's what you called your messages, right? Anna and I listened to them on her voice mail, giggling, but when she was out I rushed to put them on paper. You left those messages, knowing that I might listen to them. You suggested rendezvous to Anna, knowing that we lived together. Your love made you desperate enough to behave as if I didn't exist. It drove me out of my mind. Once I happened to be there when you called. I didn't say a word. You kept repeating: "Anna? Anna? Anna?" I hung up. What was happening to me? I went on working. Anna and I finished shooting *Cul-de-sac*. After that, I agreed to act in a short film. A small part. Anna was working like crazy. She came home late—tired and wound up. We'd talk for a while. She would fall asleep quickly. Between the silence of the night and the regular breathing of the sleeping Anna slipped in, relentlessly, the presence of Michèle.

"One night not so long ago, I got up and began to write in the notebook where I'd transcribed your messages. The next morning, after Anna had left, I opened it. The little blue mist, the one that wafts through my daydreams when I think about you, filled the room. I read what I'd written the night before. It was about you. And it was Michèle who'd written it. A Michèle who has since asserted herself. To the point where I can see her in the wig, the skirt, the makeup, to the point where I … ah, Christophe, when I saw you just now picking up the debris from your sculpture, I wanted to run away without saying goodbye. In my irritation I opened the wrong door. I was in your darkroom. I thought to myself: 'You've just broken into his Anna-Machine. This is where he enlarges it, multiplies it. You've got no business here. Get out!' But my attention was drawn to a light bulb. It cast a blue light in its corner. Next to it, another bulb, switched off and red, looked like a sleeping eye. Behind them, tacked down, a photo was buckling. I went up to look at it. It was a photo of Anna. On a beach. Behind her, the ocean. A detail caught my eye. Anna was wearing the coat from the sculpture. I'd also worn it on Halloween. At my suggestion Anna and I had traded clothes. It gave me a sensual pleasure. Just like a while ago when I found the courage to rummage in her drawers for a couple of little things I could borrow. I took the photo so I could study it. I had the impression that it was being erased before my eyes. I switched off the blue light, which left me in total darkness. I touched my face to make sure it wasn't slowly disappearing. Intending to switch on the blue bulb, I switched on the red. The room toppled into desire. I no longer needed those clothes from one night. I was going to get rid of them, meet up with you and show myself to you as I ... But I recognized Anna's voice behind the door. My heart started beating like mad. From behind the door I heard what Anna told you. She'd gone through my things. She'd read my notebook. Now she knows ... "

"You mean she recognized you just now?"

"As soon as she spotted me."

Lâm shot me a look that made me turn my head. Like an idiot, I offered him coffee. He said yes. The coffee I'd made for Anna was tepid. I threw it out, made some fresh. I tumbled down into my usual tunnel and couldn't find any solution but to pour coffee. I watched Lâm's painted face form a stain in my kitchen. A stain in the form of expectation. Why did my life always seem like a fall? I went on tumbling and couldn't get over it: Lâm, my rival, who had seduced Anna as I'd dreamed of doing, was in my kitchen, drinking my coffee—and burning with desire for me!

"Christophe, I knew you were expecting Anna tonight at the Slow-Boeing. I'd listened to the messages. I decided that Michèle would go in her place. But what was she going to say to you? I wanted to say a few words to see if they were true to the new face that the mirror sent back to me. My throat contracted. I went to the Slow-Boeing with a notepad and a pencil."

I went to the bathroom and swallowed two aspirins. Then sat down at the kitchen table again, facing Lâm. A watery smile was floating on his painted lips. Why hadn't I thrown him out? Rita's imploring face paralyzed me. I hadn't mentioned my "Mexican adventure" to anyone, not even Xenophon to whom I told everything. Wasn't I experiencing with Lâm what Rita had experienced with me? I was used to my love being turned down. But my experience in refusing love myself was slight, to say the least. Lâm had no idea of the emotion he'd triggered in me. I saw myself again brandishing the lethal knife. I lived again the stupefaction of that night which Rita had forced me to live. Had I been hypnotized by her delirium? Was I so sensitive to love bestowed on me that I was ready to do anything—and therefore the worst—in return? Hadn't the lack of love unsettled me? I told Lâm my story. It was his turn to listen to me. I found the words to bring back the astonished light cast by the moon on Eagle Cliff. I told him about Rita's ramblings, her disarming behaviour, her confession, her desperate love, her horrible request.

11

The Butterfly Fish

THAT NIGHT, at the very moment when I brought down my murderous arm with a shriek, the swarm of butterflies—very likely the same one that had brought me to my rendezvous—had swooped down brutally onto the cliff. At first I was propelled in every direction, then the ground beneath me suddenly gave way. I lost my balance. Plunged headfirst.

When I came back to my senses, my body was resting on the last steps leading to the grotto. I raised my head. A ray of sunlight searched my face. On all fours I climbed the stone staircase. Close to the entrance my hand touched something: my brace. I felt my neck. It was there. I felt my head. There also. I made it move forwards, backwards. Everything seemed normal. I found, crushed against the inner wall of the brace, a butterfly. The monarchs! All at once my memory came back. With its horrifying message: I had thrust a knife into someone's heart. What was in store for me now? Hanging. A lethal injection.

I got up to climb the last steps. Dawn greeted me, knowing nothing about my crime. Or was pretending to have come up on an ordinary day. I blinked. No trace now of the monarchs. A clear sky. I looked for Rita's dead body. It wasn't there. I touched the ground as if my eyes were lying, then I looked up towards the edge of the cliff ... and spotted her! Alive! Her back was a bright spot, motionless. I called to her. Never did a cry feel happier to me: it brought me back to the world. I called out again. She didn't budge, was upright as a statue contemplating the space at her feet. I ran to her. Was about to touch her shoulder when she turned around.

"My splatter! See how magnificent it is: the morning light is the most intelligent. It lets you see what's important. Where have you been? I thought the monarchs had kidnapped you. No, don't answer. I only asked out of kindness. Hold onto your mystery. In the sun your eyes look like a cat's."

"You aren't dead! But the knife?"

"I threw it into the sea."

"But I ... What happened yesterday?"

"Alf came back. He forgave me. Let's forget the black sound of a heart being torn out. Let's stop dancing the tango. Let's dance a waltz."

"But I ... "

"Yesterday, a gentle shower of genitals fell on us. Ah, Huachi! Listen to the breeze, it's laughing! Laughing at newborns because nothing is new. Except the sex, which purrs like a cat embedded in the sun-warmed stone. Ah, Huachi, tick-tock, no more tango, no more thighs, I laugh like the breeze, I laugh at your chicken thighs, I extract all thighs from my life, no more tango, only a blind waltz that makes its way through the sofas of sleep. Let us taste the uselessness of sex with no meat to offer, shall we? Sex in the form of tickling, sex bristling with antennae, sex that's slow to awaken, that opens, that forgets to close, that asks questions without waiting for an answer, sex in no hurry to make love, because love that is made isn't love. Love does nothing, it sexes, it sexes like the only possible verb!"

"Stop spouting nonsense! Answer me, what happened? I'm not sure of anything any more. The knife ... the butterflies ... I fell ... did I ... "

"The king of the monarchs: I saw his soul."

Rita had flung her arms towards the sky. She was shouting, ordering the monarchs to return. She was pointing to an invisible spot.

"Look, Huachi, the monarchs! Let's make love. It's the only thing that will attract them. Come back! Petals of salt! Come back!"

I was looking at a degenerate—and also an unpredictable maniac, a powerful, invincible vampire. And I was going mad. Those inoffensive butterflies wouldn't postpone tearing me to shreds. I couldn't remember, Lâm, how I came to by the side of the paved road. I see myself again waving desperately at a minibus. An hour later I'd packed my bags, I was on the wharf, anxious, afraid I'd see Rita appear, escorted by a squadron of butterflies. I took the first boat. I couldn't sit still. I was sure it would go faster if I stood and watched Isla Mujeres get smaller as we moved away from it.

A few minutes later, I turned around to get a look at the coast. Panic: we weren't going to Cancún. I jumped on the deck, shouting: "*Dónde* goes the boat? *Dónde, dónde?*" It was going to Cozumel, another island. I looked at the passengers: villagers, fishermen, merchants. Some had baskets of flowers and vegetables at their feet. They were on their way to work. They were smiling at me. They were all smiling at me. A plot was being hatched against me. All were in league to stop me from returning to Cancún. I was going to breathe my last in Cozumel, Rita and her butterflies would catch up with me. An old man gestured with his big red hand that I should sit down beside him. I fled to the other end of the boat. I heard people laughing.

They were making fun of me, probably reciting atrocities about me. And then, nothing. The wind, the sound of the waves, the vibration of the motor. I calmed down, reasoned with myself—and in the end I was the one who was mocking myself.

At Cozumel, a ferry was about to depart for Playa del Carmen. That would leave me a half-hour bus ride from Cancún. I embarked right away. To kill some time, I gawked at the rusty hull of the boat that was making its way through the water. Finally the boat docked at Playa del Carmen. It was just a small fishing village with a few hotels under construction: a tumultuous scene featuring stirred-up dust, pneumatic drills, and concrete. I was witnessing the beginning of a massacre, the massacre of a peaceful village by transforming it into a tourist centre. I spotted a row of taxis. I was incapable of looking for a bus or, worse, to wait for one, or even—and this would be worse than worse—making a mistake and boarding a bus that would very likely deliver me to Belize. I opened the door of a car: "¡*Cancún! ¡Cancún! ¡Por favor!*"

The taxi started up. A moment later I was bent double on the back seat, laughing. Uncontrollable nervous laughter. As if I'd had a narrow escape from death. The taxi-driver parked by the side of the road. He thought I was sick or stoned. I climbed out of the car. When I was finally able to catch my breath, I could make out a very simple structure with a roof of palm fronds. Fastened to a post was a wooden sign on which the words "Marlin Azul" had been carved. The sea was glittering behind it. The ribbon of beach, immaculately white, brought out the gleaming turquoise of the waves. A few widely-spaced coconut palms were gazing at infinity, adding a cry of joy to the cloudless sky. Without any warning, without my soul detecting the slightest harbinger of what was going to happen, as if the present were a material forever indecipherable and had nothing to do with the not-too-distant future, I felt in the depths of my flesh that I'd "arrived" somewhere. Precisely where the taxi had stopped, the end of the world began— the only spot where the sound of my existence, with its fear, could be silent at last.

I removed my bags from the taxi, paid the driver, and stepped under the roof of palm fronds. I saw before me some hanging corpses. I waited for my eyes to adjust to the dimness before venturing to take a few steps. I could make out, hanging from a wall, a turtle shell; an iguana skin surmounted by a jaw—its own, no doubt; a deer's hide; a crocodile's; the jaws of two sharks; some earthenware jugs. In the centre of the wall was a small niche where a wicker basket that held two bottles of ketchup stood. There were chairs with carved backs and tables. The place was used as a refectory or a restaurant. On the red-and-white tile floor lay a stuffed jaguar. In one corner, there was a big cage where two baby parrots were dreaming; I thought they were stuffed as well. Then I noticed a small counter. On it lay some greasy magazines with curled-up corners. Time had stopped. In the sea breeze drifted bits of palm fronds that dangled from the roof. Close to the pile of magazines was a sparkling bell, a small metal dome with a button on top. I hadn't seen one of those since I was a child. My first grade teacher had one sitting on a corner of her enormous desk. Whenever we were rambunctious she would punch the bell. The ringing calmed us down. The one I was looking at here was identical to the one in my memory. I struck it, but with much less confidence than my teacher. Nothing. No sound. A bell without a sound! Really! Even sound had stopped here. Then a man appeared in the doorway that opened onto the beach, his silhouette standing out against the light.

"Hi! Are you looking for something?"

An American. His accent left no doubt. His sloppy outfit clashed with the appearance of the starched Mexicans I'd seen in hotels. Late forties, bald. Rather jovial. Very laid-back. His question concerned me intimately. What did I need?

Again he asked, "Do you need something?"

"A place, a room, somewhere to stay."

"For how long?"

"I don't know."

"Okay, whatever you want."

Whatever you want. It had been an eternity since anyone said that to me. That little statement worked like a magic formula. Yes, I am doing what I want.

I followed the American along the beach. He let me carry my bags. Which was fine with me. He showed me some cabins—little white houses that blazed in the light. There were a dozen or so.

"Take whatever one you want, you're the only tourist for the moment," he said.

I picked the second-last. For no particular reason. He gave me the key and left me alone. The door had a big padlock, rusty from the sea salt. I opened it. Inside there was sand on the floor, a bed, a small wooden table, a wicker chair, and the sound of the sea. I had the sensation that in this room, I would be invisible, protected by the indifference of the universe. Rita and her monarchs would never find me here. I lay down and in spite of the afternoon light, I fell asleep. When I opened my eyes it was night. I was hungry. I waited for dawn, soothed by the breeze that was lifting the torn curtain.

I spent the first days at Marlin Azul amazed at simply being alive. Between my two eyes and my two ears, I carried a portion of the void that did me the greatest good. I vanished into the heat from the sky. My photo project resurfaced.

I took my camera out of its case. There were only the sea, the palm trees, a dusty road, scrub, crumbling cliffs, rocks licked by the waves, stunning light, sparkling shells: postcards, all of it. My Canon dropped from my hands. A few days later, I tried again. But to my great surprise I started to cry. I put my Canon back in its case and wrote a letter to the Canadian government. I denounced myself. I confessed to the people on the Canada Council for the Arts, as well as to all of Canada's taxpayers, how I had cheated. Never could I carry out successfully, as I'd submitted it, my artistic project. I discovered that the photographer in me was dead. I lost sleep. Spent my nights listening to the sound of the waves.

The events of the Night of the Butterflies came back to haunt me. I could no longer tolerate the sun. I spent my time in my little room, sweating, sweating, sweating. I was afraid of scorpions. A hundred times a day I checked my sandals, my mattress. Some Belgian tourists had taken over Marlin Azul. A couple of German women too. I fled, tried to eat the small amount of food my stomach could tolerate at impossible hours, to be sure that I'd be alone in the restaurant. In the end, I admitted it to myself: my thoughts were all of Rita.

I stopped shaving. I had no centre, no nail on which to hang the frame of my experiences. I was dripping. An image was pursuing me: the head of the angel. I relived the moment when I'd found myself face to face with it in the grotto. After several nights of insomnia, of questioning, of moral stagnation, I gave in. It had been a dream. Nothing had happened. Maybe I really had met a woman on the beach in Cancún. Maybe she looked like a man. No doubt some details had alarmed me, a hint of beard under the nose, overly powerful shoulders, the absence of curves here and there, nothing more. We'd argued a little. At most, had a drink or two. She'd told me the story of her life: small pieces, nothing out of the ordinary. And then we had parted: because of weariness, because of some banal reason, because it was late, because the daytime sun had softened us. The rest was an excrescence that had grown on I know not what trunk. I was not a tree. It wasn't me who'd imagined it.

The next day, everything toppled over again. My mind rejected these ravings, brought me back to square one: it had all happened. I finally wore down reality by casting it in doubt, by turning it over and over in every direction, by sticking my finger into its holes. I no longer saw the sea and its green infinity, no longer heard the living sound of its waves. Rita's ghost had replaced Anna's. It wouldn't let go of me. Then one night I understood the significance of my torments: I had wanted to kill someone. I, Christophe, had the soul of a murderer. My reason refused to admit it, preferring to convince me that I'd dreamed. What had happened that night? Had I really tried to plunge a knife into someone's heart? Had I done it? Yet Rita was alive. My mind became confused. I had to see this story through to the end. Three weeks after coming to Marlin Azul, I decided to go back to Isla Mujeres.

Before I left, I threw myself into the sea to bid it farewell. Splashed around, did a few breast-strokes. Then stopped. Someone was biting my leg. Someone? No, a sawfish, a shark. I understood the meaning of "to take to one's heels," an expression I personified quite precisely. On the sand, I went into a furious dance. I hadn't been bitten. Outside the water, what I felt was a burn on my right thigh. I examined it. It looked normal. A Belgian tourist came up to me, alerted by my cries and my experimental dance. I explained what had happened. She sat me down, inspected my thigh, let out a victory cry. She pointed to some red spots that had just appeared on my skin. As a result, I felt better. I wasn't crazy. I really was suffering. Three other tourists, also Belgians, came up to me. I was examined again. My red patches were growing. My thigh was swelling up. A lively discussion followed. The verdict was in: I had been in contact with a jellyfish. They reassured me. It wasn't fatal. The irritation would go away on its own. A little moisturizing cream would do no harm. After all, jellyfish have to express themselves, don't they? I thanked them, took to my heels again. It was time to leave Marlin Azul.

I got to the Cancún bus station. Hurled myself at a travel agency. Before going back to Isla Mujeres, I wanted to be sure I had a return flight to Montreal. The next one would take off in two days. I left my bags in a locker, and took a taxi to Puerto Juárez where I embarked again on the ferry that shuttled back and forth between the coast and Isla Mujeres. And there I was, with pounding heart, on the island's cursed soil.

Why hadn't I just stayed still in a Cancún hotel room, staring at the hours one by one, at the minutes even—counting them, checking them—to be sure they were mounting up properly and that there would be no delay, nothing to interfere with my plane's take-off? Some lugubrious power inhabited me, no doubt. Like a robot's, my footsteps took me back to the Hotel Rosario. I studied its brightly-coloured façade. Yes, I had slept there. Why press the point? I went to the motorbike shop. Again, I could hear my heartbeats. The boy was going to recognize me as the bike thief, would alert the police. And I'd end up in jail. I would die a virgin, gnawed by rats. I slowed down. The boy was indeed at his post. He returned my smile. Relieved, I continued on to the cemetery. Walked through the gate. As if I were a regular on the premises, I turned left. The one I was looking for was there. His head had been put back. I knelt. In the blinding light of noon I addressed the angel: "She will come, won't she? She comes at three o'clock every afternoon. I'll wait for her here. I have to talk to her, I ... I can't go on living with that idea, that sensation ... Did I really try to ... "

I fell silent. I'd just heard whispering. I turned around: no one, only graves, sand, and unbearable heat. I came closer to the angel. Was he speaking to me? His white lips weren't moving. A weird thought went through me: what if Rita were walled up inside? I pressed my ear against the statue. The mumbling was transformed into a distinct series of words.

" ... nearly killed you. I should have killed you. Too late. You're dead. You exposed me to every insult ... The butterflies! The butterflies! How many times, hiding from Mama, did you tell me that story to put me to sleep ... The butterflies! On the phone you said: 'Come and join me in Mexico, make an effort, you'll look after my funeral, I need you.' Need me! You never thought about me as a human. To you, I was ... I was ... Actually, what was I to you? When you told me the doctors had said it was hopeless, I thought it was another of your traps. The things you've made up! I'm telling you: when I realized a mouse was nibbling at your brain, I couldn't stop myself from dancing. At last I'll be able to ... "

I'd walked around the angel. There really was someone talking to me, but not from inside the statue, simply behind it. I recognized it right away: Andy. The boy with the Polaroid. The one who didn't know that John Lennon had been one of the Beatles. He was sitting, half hidden by the sand, leaning listlessly against the statue's pedestal, holding a Corona, wearing yellow boxers, bare-chested, wet with sweat, spotted, his usually pink face scarlet. At least a dozen empty beer bottles surrounded him like a funeral wreath. He didn't see me right away. He went on talking, head hanging.

"Are you really Andy?"

Slowly, he brought up his head, looked at me with no surprise.

"He was right. He swore that you'd come back. My father was always right."

"Your father?"

Andy threw the bottle he'd been holding into the sky, tried to stand up, fell back onto the sand, tried again, propping himself against the statue, and stood up, his back to me. What was he doing now? I thought he'd turned away from me to cry. I approached him. He turned around abruptly. He was pissing.

"His last moments were excruciating. He didn't miss a single chance to put me on the spot. He imposed on me the spectacle of his death. Today, I'm watering his funeral. I'm sure he's happy, he's buried next to his angel."

Still pissing, Andy moved closer to me. I was disoriented. Rita was dead and I was discovering that she had a son.

"So here you are again!"

"Me?"

"The fish."

"The fish?"

"The butterfly."

"The butterfly?"

"The butterfly fish. That was how he talked about you to me. He got you, eh? You know what? I published a book at the age of fifteen. A true story. I had plenty to say. I was on TV. I didn't name my father, didn't accuse him, but I gave him a scare. And how! It was important to me. And seemed fair enough under the circumstances. My mother kicked him out. They'd hated each other for ages. Asshole that I was, I was starting to have some regrets. I wept and wailed for him for a while. Don't look at me like that, my father told me the whole story, he got your number the first time he laid eyes on you, he really got you good, didn't he, he was brilliant, my father, but not an easy man to get along with, not nice, mean, jealous, envious— a godsend! The tales he could tell! It gave me a taste of life that was hard to swallow. What do you think I've turned into—a genius, a plumber, a psychopath? Nothing, absolutely nothing, I tell you, I'm nothing. Do you know why? Because I'm totally satisfied, and when you're totally satisfied you feel obliged to be happy, otherwise nothing makes any sense, so I'm a Buddhist. Don't laugh, I really am a Buddhist. It feels so good to say it, but that's all, you know, once it's said it's already in the past, because I'm not a Buddhist any more, it's just that I thought about it, imagine, you make your mind go blank, you lighten up as they say in the Himalayas, how do you expect me to lighten up when I've got that between my legs? You want the truth? I'm seventeen, it's all I think about. I'm like him, he implanted it under my fingernails. The things he said to convince me that I was one of the chosen! Ah, precocious, precocious, it's so good when it's precocious, when it's puke green, when it's fresh, insignificant, and Zen in the middle, like a spiral candy, and it makes you so bright and anaesthetized! You understand everything, you stop questioning yourself. Sex, you know what, sex is the ultimate answer, the cosmic cork, it shuts the yap to infinity, what else do you want afterwards, afterwards you just want to start again. A tic, not a nervous one, not cardiac, a tic from God, yes, Huachi, it's God in the form of a tic! You're itchy, you fry in oil, you fidget. My father was brilliant, but he was a son-of-a-bitch. We fought over you, you know, I'm sure he never whispered in your ear that he had a son, that it bothered him. Since my scandalous book came out, my papa with the thousand hands never touched me, he avoided me for a year. I expected it, mind you, but I suffered, what was I saying ... I was saying that ... ah, yes, my father and I fought because of you, you understand, I was against it, when he told me he'd flushed out a fish I told him he was crazy, he was at death's door, it was not the moment to have it off with you. Huachi here, Huachi there, he stood by his fish. The crap he could say to entice you, he's brilliant, my father, brilliant, he should have made movies instead of wasting his time in the import-export business ... "

"Wasn't he an engineer?"

Andy, who, luckily for me, had finally stopped pissing, obviously hadn't heard my question and he kept going, arms flung up to heaven.

" ... at least he made a bundle, I'm rich now—and that's the problem. What am I going to do with my money? It makes me sad, I'm too generous, I have to restrain myself from giving it all away to the first person who turns up. You don't believe me? Fine, think what you want, be my guest, it proves that you're ordinary. Can you imagine a worse fate for a man than to be ordinary? You see, you seem to agree with me: being ordinary removes the salt from salt, the sugar from sugar, that's bullshit, sorry, aren't you tempted, a good-looking guy like me, with pecs of steel, you want to know my secret?"

With that, Andy flopped onto the sand like a sack. I thought he'd fainted. I rushed over to help while wondering what kind of help he would need. I bent over him. Moving briskly, Andy had grabbed my arm and, with incredible strength, flung me to the ground.

"Huachi here, Huachi there. True, you aren't bad. I like your green eyes. Especially when the sun sinks into them. Turns them yellow. You wouldn't be a bit diabolical, would you? You see how awkward I am with you, I don't know how to handle you. I was jealous, I admit it. You can understand that, my father makes me come to Mexico, he's going to die, he's stuffed with drugs, he doesn't want to go back to France, this is where he wants to breathe his last, close to his angel, he puts on a hell of a show, I'm sure he's lost his mind but I get on a plane and come here anyway, I land, and who do I see but him—it's him, but disguised as a babe, a clown, he tries to explain, but who gives a shit about his explanations, I'm helping him, it's normal, and I can't stand it when things are done badly, I'm a sensitive guy, so I fix him up, I put on his makeup properly, he becomes beautiful, acceptable, fit to be seen, I'm quite proud of playing that trick on my crazy old man, of making him a total woman, it excites me, makes me crazy, then in my hotel room that night, I have a good cry, call myself a savage, I'm disgusted, I want to slit my wrists, finally I watch some Mexican TV, try to figure out what's happening to us, but it's pitch black, and it's always there, sex, that's eating me from the inside, it's hopeless, just looking at my father to see what the future has in store for me, and then you show up with your cute little face like an over-the-hill teenager, my father makes himself even more beautiful, I really think he's losing it, but deep down I'm jealous, I came to Mexico to be with him unto death, that's how he put it, not me, to be with him unto death, and meanwhile the son-of-a-bitch comes on to you as if he was twenty again—and as a woman, no less ... "

Andy had stood up and wedged me between his legs. I could see his face bent over me, distorted, and puffy from booze. His long blond hair, wet with sweat, covered part of his eyes.

" ... but I hadn't understood a thing, I was miles from the truth, how could I know what was being cooked up inside my demented father's rotten head, can you tell me? Basically, my father deceived me; maybe he'd never forgiven me for my success, but after all, at the age of fifteen I did sell a hundred thousand copies of *My Childhood, That Disaster*. True I didn't write it all by myself, my psychologist helped out. For that matter, he helped himself by using my services, but that's another story I'll tell you when you've had some more experience of life. No, the more I think about it, the more I believe that my father didn't appreciate the fact that I talked about the part he'd played in turning my childhood into an endless experiment, otherwise he wouldn't have acted the way he did, especially on the eve of his death, he wouldn't have hidden that ... "

Andy had executed a surprising about-turn. As a result, he had his back to me and, on all fours, he was picking up the bottles lying around in the sand, sucking the last drops of beer from them. His lemon shorts made a comical spot, but I didn't feel like laughing.

" ... not hidden that fabulous project, did you know who it was intended for, what he intended for you, you little lump of modelling clay? He'd chosen you for a grandiose role, you had what it took—Greek nose, bus-stop look, and most of all, your stinking naïveté and revolting lack of judgement, and your putrid, tiresome, scandalous virginity, which sent my poor pop over the edge. He'd intended to have his heart torn out by some moron like you, my father had sex appeal, he didn't want to croak for no good reason, like a lump in a hospital bed, wrists swollen from morphine. I know he told you those stories about sacrifice, they were what kept him alive, just enough to lead him to the death he'd chosen for himself, a death offered to a sky pitted with stars. He told me—they were his last words—that he couldn't imagine a better destiny than to receive the fatal blow from the hand of a virgin, that he wanted to reverse the process, you understand, not send a virgin to the sacrificial altar but give him the knife so he could lift it and then bring it down onto his pitiful life, onto his sin, his remorse, his stupidity. He could never forgive himself for missing the rendezvous with Alfred, never. That dazzled me, gave me a stomach ache, I had to go to the toilet, when I came back he was smiling peacefully, tears in the corner of his eyes, he told me the final instalment, Alfred's ghost coming to whisper forgiveness in person, total madness, he told me in his weakened voice: 'Andy, dear Andy, Alfred is back, I thought I would join him in death, he came to me twenty years after his death, in the dark night of my life, it's his heart that I heard beating at the heart of that storm of heartbeats, the monarchs conveyed his gaze all the way to mine, Huachi brought up his arm, he shouted, I saw the king of the monarchs gliding over my pathetic life, I was able to gaze at the soul of my beloved, he came to say that he forgave me, I turned away, the blade of the knife brushed against me.' Do you know what I think? Let me tell you, it doesn't hold water, who do you think I am to swallow a story like that, no, definitely, I can't wrap my mind around such a thing, surely you don't expect me to believe that crap about the butterflies that boom, peekaboo, looky looky, we're pretty pairs of wings, Alfred sent us, he wanted us to tell you he's hale and hearty, twenty years earlier he'd very much enjoyed executing a swan dive, he broke some bones but in the end—because everything, fortunately, comes to an end—it's to his advantage, lets him play superhero, prevent some horrible, pointless crime and, most of all, to forgive, yes, that's the word: to forgive. My crazy old man died at that point, totally forgiven, sure he'd be going to heaven where he'd wind himself around his rotten Alf. But who do you think I am, you monstrous virgin with the knot in his prick? I know what happened that night on the Eagle Cliff, there was no super-boom of butterflies, no crappy apparition, no—what's the word?—no epiphany, that's the goddamn word, no epiphany with all its garbage about redemption, you know, like, it's the end of the film, bring on the violins, the twilight lighting, the spectator, bound to his piss-soaked chair, is about to squeeze a tear out of his filthy incontinent glands, a tear, proof that he's ready to go, too ready, even! No, there was none of that 'super' shit stuffed with stars because it was you, admit it, it was you who didn't have the balls to hit my father smack in the heart like he'd asked you so nicely to do, you're the shit-disturber, the gutless wonder that didn't take this grandiose story to the bitter end! You don't deserve to have a prick, you should have been born without an ass, as round as a golf ball, a circus spectacle put on display in the dreary light of some ramshackle tents. Do you know what you did? You deprived my father of his death, the death he'd dreamed about for twenty years, the death he must have imagined thousands of times, turned over and over in his aching head. He needed that death if he was going to die as he'd lived. And at the last moment you stole it from him. What was it you said to him, did to him, to make him believe that half-baked doo-doo about the butterflies, to send him into the most mind-boggling hallucinations, to make him feel absolved of his crime without really paying the price? I'm the one who should have been holding the knife, who should've skewered him in his good-for-nothing heart, who should have consoled him till the end of time. You usurped my place, you robbed me of my father, you robbed me of his death, you stole my murder! Who are you—green eyes, weak thighs, Huachinango, who are you, you dork? You didn't have the balls to see it through, to kill, just to kill, it's like love, isn't it, like sex, what do you deserve, will you tell me?"

Andy missed. He'd just tossed me a bottle of beer. Stunned by the sun but even more by the flood of words that had just exited his mouth like an endless snake, I took off, fearing that the worst was yet to come. Despite his intoxication—or because of it—Andy grabbed me, flung me to the ground, yanked my hair, my nose, stuck a finger in my nostril, pinched my cheeks.

"I'm not angry. I approve of what you did. It may not look that way. I'm young, please excuse me, I'm not used to subtleties, give me a couple of years, I'll be as predictable as a politician. You pulled a very big thorn from my paw, probably you didn't even know it, but hey, who cares about what we know, if we know what we know because we know it, or because it's known somewhere inside us without our knowing it. Basically I would not have liked to find my father's corpse at the bottom of a creek, torn to pieces and minus the heart. Can you imagine the problems, the awkwardness, the never-ending hassle with the cops? Already they've come chasing after me, because of you actually. They mistook me for you, another judicial error. Apparently there's a resemblance. I did time in jail because of you, for the theft of a motorbike, I had to pay, but I'm rich now, I won't ask you to reimburse me, I've got class, I've got a heart, in fact they finally admitted they'd made a mistake but they kept my money anyway. In my opinion they thought we were together—brothers, friends, or something else. After all, it was me who took you to the hospital, unconscious, beautiful as a pile of coal and little daisies. You arranged that on purpose, didn't you? You played dead, or at least severely injured. I'm sure there was nothing wrong with you. Do you know what you are? A green-eyed pervert, the worst kind. And I'm sincerely glad that you're back. I couldn't believe it. Before he died, my father swore you'd come back to the cemetery to visit him one last time. He was intuitive, I'm not. I'm leaving tomorrow, putting Mexico behind me, I'm turning the page, erasing it, pulling it out, swallowing it! I treated myself to a little party of my own, as you can see, I've made my farewells, I've pissed on his grave so much that he can smell it, a friendly little act of revenge. Sincerely, I insist on repeating it, I'm no skinflint, I'm glad you're here, that way I can thank you, you were his last delight, he told me so. I'm not really jealous of you, I wanted to impress you, and the more I think of it, the more it seems to me that if you hadn't turned up, I would have killed my father, yes, killed him, and not the way he'd asked, not with the whole lovely horror film by a beginner, I had my own plan that was less romantic. I just wanted to cut off his prick and make him eat it! After that, he'd have been free to die his own death, one that was gentle, slow, anticipated, hurried, slowed down by drugs. In fact I wouldn't have killed him, only messed him up, then we would've been even, both of us messed up. Do you see how you kept me from committing an odious act, you're an angel too, you've come at the right time, you deserve something, you came here for a reason, you're looking for something and you're going to get it, look, help yourself, I'm your angel, why are you closing your eyes, why not look at the fruit platter I'm offering you? It's free for once!"

Andy was crazy. He disgusted me. He was shamelessly putting on a show. He reeked of beer and piss. I pitched a fistful of sand in his eyes. He howled in pain. I managed to push him off me, I fled the cemetery, ran without turning around. Unable to wait for the next ferry I rented a small boat to take me back to Cancún. I collected my bags, took a taxi to the airport. My plane wouldn't leave for another thirty hours but I preferred to sit in a chair and twiddle my thumbs to the bones, flash-frozen by the air-conditioning, than spend another day in Cancún. At the airport it felt as if Mexico now existed in a less virulent form, that part of me, the most vulnerable part, had already left. I was terrified that Andy would turn up. Hadn't he said in his raving that he was leaving Mexico too? I figured that with my luck, I was liable to end up on the same plane, in the next seat. Till the last moment I expected to see him walk in, still wearing his disgusting boxers, dragging suitcases full of Corona behind him. For once, though, the worst didn't happen. I was on the verge of happiness when I boarded the plane at the appointed time. Rita was dead. Never again would I think about her.

It was during takeoff that the first symptoms of fever appeared. Initially, I thought it was my emotion at the prospect of going home. But after an hour of my teeth chattering, I had to face up to it. I was sick—fever, vomiting. I went through customs at Mirabel with a pumpkin in place of a head. During the flight, some golfball-sized ganglia had sprouted in my armpits. My leg, the one the jellyfish had burned with its secretions, had doubled in size. At least that was how it felt when I tried to move it so I could tread at last the ground of Montreal, and then the dusty floor of my apartment where I crashed like a Boeing, weeping tears I didn't know I had in me, noting that I was no happier at home than where I'd come from, that hell was everywhere, that I was coming apart like a puddle, overlooked by the universe. No one knew I was home, not even Xenophon. I could peacefully croak on the spot, in absolute peace. But already the four-letter ghost was insisting on having its share. I loved, I loved Anna. I had to love her! Without that love I was nothing. Not much more than a mouth that could still pronounce the two magic syllables of *Anna*, as if that mouth had detached itself from the rest of my body, leaving the site of a disaster so that, in the nick of time, she could save the essential—a small suitcase of love: two whispering lips.

I had to see a number of doctors before I gave up. Who could put down on paper, with the official ink of scientific certainty, what I'd brought home from Mexico—not in my bags but in my blood? The jellyfish had injected me with a virus. That was the least vague version I could fall back on. I was sick. Now I wasn't. Sick again. My leg was back to normal, but the fever—lashing, distorting reality—would hit without warning. I wandered around my apartment, moving nothing but balls of dust that bounced like bunnies. My allergy to dust, to smells, had lost all importance. I sneezed, unconcerned. What did those mundane details matter to me? I concentrated on just one thing: loving Anna. And it was in the throes of my fever that I wrote the first lines of my *annalexicon*. It did nothing for me, Lâm, as you could see. Anna never came to our rendezvous.

"I did."

"More coffee? I'm out of milk."

At which point I fainted. Again.

Part Three

BEAUTY FALLEN FROM THE SKY

12

Xenophon's Baby Toes

TO MY AMAZEMENT, I received a letter from the Canada Council for the Arts. I'd forgotten that Canada existed. I'd forgotten that art existed and even had its very own Council. I'd also forgotten that I'd once been a photographer. I allowed myself a brief moment of nostalgia. Because of the letter. It was a reply to one I'd written, which I'd also forgotten about, in which I called myself a hole of varying circumference because sorrow, that spongy material, couldn't correctly set the limits of its jurisdiction. And plenty of other senseless remarks. The person who'd signed the letter congratulated me on my intellectual honesty, suggested I see a health-care professional, advised me that I would be granted an extension to permit me to delve deeper into my artistic interrogation within the context of some new parameters. I tore it up. "New parameters!" What am I, Christophe Langelier, if not a pile of new parameters? All ills come from our fixation with wanting come hell or high water to resemble ourselves, while every second of our existence draws us towards other roads, other suns, other mirrors. An accomplishment I'm proud of: at this moment, I no longer resemble myself. Tomorrow, even less so!

But what had happened to make those remarks fall from my mouth? Living for myself came under the jurisdiction not of the obvious, but of a wager constantly won, lost, won again, lost again—till the gambler and even the final result were exhausted. It hardly mattered what was added or subtracted, everything gravitated towards a lugubrious zero that was swallowing me.

Lâm was staying at my place now. He'd made sure that Anna wasn't home before picking up his things to bring them over. They saw each other every day however because *Cul-de-sac II* was in production following the unexpected and colossal success of *Cul-de-sac*, which immediately begat a sequel that in Lâm's opinion would be ludicrous, tasteless, and implausible—but bound to enjoy an even unhealthier vogue with the public. Anna and Lâm had become stars overnight, fresh meat for a hungry public. They were recognized on the street, they were on the covers of all the magazines. They turned down interviews and TV appearances: too busy. They embodied the couple. They were Romeo and Juliet on Saint-Laurent Boulevard. But they were also Lâm and Anna and that infuriated me.

For me too, events followed thick and fast. I was the subject of a metamorphosis that disgusted me profoundly. While most of the symptoms that had appeared on the plane had quickly gone, except for the fever, others had taken over. They'd appeared on the morning after the night when Lâm and I, over three pots of coffee, had told each other the stories of our lives until I fell down, he put me to bed and then, on observing the first signs of my spectacular metamorphosis, decided to devote himself to the monster I was becoming. And far from scared, discouraged, or sickened, he was delighted, amused, excited. Why was Lâm behaving that way? He had imposed his presence. He'd trapped me at the Slow-Boeing. I had behaved with him like a grain of sand that thinks, as it trickles through the hourglass, that it is escaping confusion, when in fact it is diving into another pile of it, cancelling out again its little grey dot. Lâm still loved Anna. He'd told me so again, but that didn't stop him, he said with a hint of a smile, from loving someone else, thereby proffering a double dose of love. In matters of the heart, Lâm didn't add, he multiplied. I was in such a state that I let him. I mean let him love me, care for me, live with me, only see Anna at work, resign himself to the loss of his love, swear to me that I didn't make him feel like vomiting. Because I'd become repulsive. I lost pieces of skin just by raising my arm. My sheets creaked under this build-up of gigantic dandruff. Around my mouth and in my eyes, a substance accumulated that I couldn't identify. Why did Lâm take pleasure in washing that sticky face? In spoon-feeding me? In cutting my hair that had become a field of wild grasses? I was so aloof from everything, especially from the present, that I was unable to question myself about what was happening to me. The fact that Lâm had taken a spoon to scrape up the lumps that had collected between my fingers, my toes, in my ears and elsewhere did not in itself merit comment, judgement, the pallor of surprise. I was nothing. Merely a tiny self hidden in folds of flesh, smothered, a hole that the thread of my existence just squeaked through, relieved of ideas about oneself, others, the world. I'd never taken such a radical look at myself: one look too many and I drowned in the air. I had doused all the flames of desire, of yearning, of the things that life makes us do, to send us sooner to our death. I had nothing left to lose, nothing left to gain.

I spent three weeks stuck to my sheets, merged with my mattress. One morning I sensed that I could do it: I got up, went up to the bathroom mirror. Earlier, Lâm had brought me a small one so I could discover, bit by bit, the new bumps on my epidermis. How had Lâm been able to touch me, caress me, talk to me, how had he been able to relinquish Anna's radiant beauty to come and take care of all that? What was he—star of the moment, hero with the honey-coloured skin—doing here with me? I wanted to call Xenophon. He was the only other friend I had. If I told him just a tenth of what I was going through he'd come running, bang my head against the kitchen wall, wake me from my nightmare, confirm that it was Tuesday. Someone had to rescue me. I punched in his number. A recorded message told me it was not in service. Where was he? I should have contacted him as soon as I was back from Mexico. I hadn't even sent him a postcard to prove that I was a serious, recognized visual artist eligible for travel grants. My inability to talk with Xenophon, whose existence I'd forgotten for months, became a matter of life and death. I was devastated. "I can't talk to Xenophon!" I howled into the telephone. I felt as if I'd just been voted Orphan of the Universe. I was nothing but a solitary monster because a phone number I'd called was being answered by the doldrums, the void, the unknown. I consumed cereal—a whole box of it—with milk and bananas. Lâm had bought bananas. Then the weight of the earth toppled over.

Anna echo, Anna wave, Anna dose, Anna zoo, Anna blast, Anna skin, Anna embargo, Anna catastrophe. Anna, I hate you!

It happened like that, like a reflux of vitamin-packed cereal. Who are you, Anna? I'd never asked myself that. In the beginning, Anna had been born from a star, had descended to earth on little pink feet that allowed her to float instead of walk. Inside her body there were no slimy, stinky organs. Oh, no! Two magnificent magnolias were her lungs. A rose pumped her blood. A basin lined with rushes took in her food and digested it with a gurgle of happy bubbles. A pine tree, slender and evergreen, kept her erect but supple. As for her sex, my imagination threw in the towel. Anna's sex was the origin of the world, the eye, the sky, the eye of the needle that, once passed through, gives access to the light. I granted her all virtues, all powers. Yes, Anna, who are you? Without the lexicon I've devoted to you, how could I possibly talk about you? Right now I hate you. Hating you gives me other words. Basically, Anna, you are an island, a little pile of selfishness dampened by an ocean of indifference where I'm concerned. When we lived together, no one but you was alive. If you'd at least deigned to notice, to take a quick and emotional look at the little dog you obliged me to become. A little dog? No, not that! A dog follows its master everywhere, shifting around its tail billions of vibrations, filling space with a joy that's idiotic but alive. But me! Yes, Anna, who are you to make me envy the fate of a dog? A malicious being, an illusion, a spoilt child, a TV star. I vomit on you! Anna carpet, Anna ad, Anna nail, Anna jeans, Anna tooth, Anna cage, Anna wall, Anna knick-knack, Anna butter, Anna broom—yes, Anna broom who sweeps the debris of my love into a corner to keep it out of your way—I hate you the same way I loved you!

There was a bomb in my mouth. One more word, one more *Anna*, and it would explode. I pursed my lips. What had I just done? I'd sullied Anna. Claimed to hate her. I truly was a monster, inside and out. I wanted forgiveness, now. Call Anna? She'd never answer. And anyway she was shooting *Cul-de-sac II*. Go to the location? How could I turn up in front of Anna? I'd become so hideous. I knelt in front of the TV. Kissed the screen. A repeat episode of *Cul-de-sac* would be on in fifteen minutes. Ever since I'd decided, after seeing the first three episodes, not to watch it, I'd been able to avoid turning it on. I even avoided the living room, afraid that the TV would come on by itself and follow me, its jaws dripping images like a bulldog slobbering onto its master's legs. But I had just profaned Anna, just vomited on my love for her. Now I must make atonement. I had to kneel down and watch Isabelle, Anna's character, declare her love for another, who is none other than Lâm, disguised as a visible minority; I had to watch her take off her T-shirt, offer her breasts and worse, watch her heart that was beating inside her. It was the least I could do for her after my disgraceful behaviour. Behaving as if Anna, behind the screen, was going to see me watching her, I switched on the TV.

Feverishly, I waited for 8:00 P.M., the fatal hour. The opening credits were just starting. I lost my nerve. Zapped. It was too much: I simply couldn't watch *Cul-de-sac*. I pressed my face against the TV screen. When I moved away, there was a small spot of blood on a public service announcement. I thought that the TV set, like certain statues, was starting to ooze, to bleed as a sign to me. But no, it was coming from my nose. I got a Kleenex. Wiped my nose. Wiped off the TV. That was when I recognized the voice of Xenophon. He was talking to a reporter who'd stuck a mike under his beard. The last time I'd seen Xenophon he was clean-shaven. What a change! He'd also let his hair grow. But his voice was the same, nasal and drawling. He was telling the reporter that he didn't deserve any credit, that he thought, yes, like everyone else, times were tough, especially for the young, but that from laziness and by definition, times were always tough and that if as bad luck would have it they let themselves go limp, it would be a disaster; that he could see the disaster very clearly, you didn't need to be a forecasting genius to sense it on the doorstep, ready to ring the bell, come in, take over people's daily lives, spill a pan of scalding soup over their heads, disfigure their kitchens with obscene graffiti, rip their Sunday lampshades with invisible claws; but that, yes, the sun always shone for the pure of heart, and his message could be held in the palm of a child's hand ...

What was Xenophon talking about? The camera plunged to his feet: he was barefoot in the cold autumn rain. That was when I noticed he had on some kind of cape from which his arms emerged, also bare. When Xenophon wasn't talking, he smiled. Gratuitously. This was quite unlike him. Next came a montage with Xenophon's face as a medallion, his eyes staring at I-don't-know-what in the distance. The report was showing us a day in the life of Xenophon. We saw him strolling, still barefoot, along Sainte-Catherine Street, followed by beggars, young people, even dogs. A priest testified: "Ever since he arrived in the neighbourhood people have been coming to Mass." A municipal councillor claimed that he couldn't forbid Xenophon's behaviour: "He does nothing illegal. Let's wait and see." In voice-over, the reporter insisted: "This young man, who calls himself Come-Back-to-Me, speaks to us of love. He asks for nothing in return. He lives on the street and considers it acceptable to feed himself, as he puts it without irony, on whatever the generous leave in their garbage cans for the destitute children of this world. Witnesses have declared they've been healed by nothing more than his touch." We then saw an old woman, accompanied by a middle-aged man, her son perhaps, grasp Xenophon's hands and lay them on her head. The voice-over went on: "Is Come-Back-to-Me a visionary (images appeared of young Hare Krishnas, skipping and chanting, accosting people on the street) or a genuine voice? It's for you to decide." The small medallion suddenly grew bigger, filling the whole screen. Xenophon was looking at me intensely: "I am what I am, I am Come-Back-to-Me."

A shampoo commercial let me catch my breath. My stomach gave out a long lament that ended in a rumbling. I'd become nothing more than an amalgam of ugliness, like car bodies that are compacted and tossed into automobile graveyards. I curled up under the kitchen table, the only place where I could disappear from the world. Seeing Xenophon on TV like that a few minutes after trying to get him on the phone, was just one of those coincidences that the world loves to produce in its spare time, thereby challenging with humour the smoothness of its operation. Or it was a sequences of events that, ever since Mexico, had been arranging my footsteps to lead me ... to lead me where? Wasn't I thinking of something set in motion by other thoughts that weren't necessarily mine? Is it an illusion to believe that man begins at birth? When our eyes close, perhaps they're only opening onto another, older world. Ever since my flight from the cemetery on Isla Mujeres, escaping Andy's sordid words and gestures, I had tried hard to crush beneath a slab of cement everything that had happened to me there. I'd gone so far as to offer myself sincere congratulations because the announcement of Rita's death, both on the spot and several days later, had produced in me not even a hint of an emotion: no tears, no nostalgia, no regret. But suddenly, as I lay there curled up in a ball, I understood something: wasn't I actually experiencing my grief over Rita? And the disease that had transformed me into a monster: wasn't it my way to mourn my dead? Wasn't I, after all, becoming more and more like a cadaver myself?

I put on a coat, pulled up the collar, and went out to look for Xenophon. I was grateful for the wind that was whipping me and putting my thoughts in some order. Yes!

Yes, I told myself, everything is connected, after one step, another, after one beat, another, and so on; without the first step, no second step; without the second, no next one. I walked the streets of Montreal that night at the speed of a man in a hurry. I passed through the summits of human thought, beyond common sense, went to the other side of things seen and heard, I retraced the history of humanity, I agreed to be part of it, to add my little bit to the endless march of beings and things, of dead and living, of objects and ideas. I thought that I could feel, in the movement of my legs as they propelled me forward, the meaning of life, the jolt of the train of meat and flowers that life carts along. Why yes, Xenophon, of course, Xenophon—and all those men and women who are at this moment breathing, trampling the earth, the sky, the sea, the air with their hands, their eyes, their feet—you, they, I, all of us are moving restlessly in the same huge, grotesque second, a drop of time immediately diluted into another that is immeasurable, stubborn, gorged with mystery and brightness because everything is connected in the bread of the world, like the legs of error and the legs of truth that have danced together since the beginning of time. Why yes, Xenophon, dear Xenophon, everything is connected, we were inseparable, one day you introduced me to Anna, she was in the year-end show at the little secondary school we attended, you'd asked me to take photos, not of the actor but of the set you'd built, but I only took photos of her, of Anna, who was playing Nina, Chekhov's poor Seagull, who stretched out her life dismally by playing unrewarding roles in sordid theatres. And how Anna made me cry that night, how moved I was when Treplev, who was crazy about Nina, crazy about Anna, killed himself, blew his own brains out; it was at that very moment that my love, a painful architect and unbounded builder, had laid the first stone of the cathedral Anna; at the very moment when Treplev was dying, my love for Anna was born, meteoric and ruthless—all that, of course, I learned later, some days later when I developed the photos from the show, it was only when I saw again Anna's face, fixed in the silence of the darkroom which the school made available to students, that love revealed itself totally, irremediably, forever embedded in my pupils; to watch as Anna appeared on the pure white photographic paper was and will always be the greatest joy of my life, the emotion that will have shaken my heart enough to detach it from its beating; yes, Xenophon, everything is connected, even the weird set you'd created for *The Seagull*, which confirmed once and for all your claim to be a stage designer; because no one, except me, obviously, had understood your idea of setting the play in a hybrid, non-identifiable, slightly repulsive place made out of recycled materials—plastic, plywood, posters, pieces of furniture that had been deconstructed, even smashed up—which clashed with the fin de siècle atmosphere of a bourgeois Russia, but expressed so clearly the inner decline of the characters and announced with prophetic force the turn my own life would take, yes, Xenophon, hadn't you understood all that when, with an insouciance that was most likely feigned, you had quickly, in a corridor of the school, introduced me to Anna, saying: "This is Anna, she plays Nina in the play, come and see her." Yes, Xenophon, I'll go and see her, see *her*, and that night, walking through the streets of Montreal in search of Xenophon, I recalled the details of that period of my life with cruel sharpness, and each memory was wrapped around another to the point of smothering it, and then making it emerge even more forcefully, creating a spiral that swept me into an agony of words; and it was in the midst of that excitement that I found Xenophon, sitting ramrod straight on a bench in Saint-Louis Square, with the vacuous smile he'd worn in the news report, leading one to believe that he hadn't budged since I'd switched off the TV.

I stood in front of him and showed him my gangrenous face, as if by displaying myself like that I wouldn't need words, the first glance would tell him everything. I expected a volley of questions or some outburst that might suggest a renewal of our friendship. But Xenophon was content to pronounce listlessly, "How about that, it's the Bicycle Eater." That was the only thing my best friend could come up with in the presence of a physical and mental deterioration as resounding as mine. He caused to appear, from where I don't know, a cellophane-wrapped sandwich. He took forever to remove the protective film, as if he were peeling some delicate fruit. Xenophon's sandwich was tuna and most likely not very fresh. Carefully, he broke off a piece and offered it to me. Thick mayonnaise was dripping from the squashed bread. Xenophon stuffed what was left of the sandwich into his mouth and, practically without chewing, gulped it down with a strange sound that for no explicable reason made me sad. He then caused a cigarette butt to appear, which he lit with the flick of a Bic. He ran his hand through my hair. I was able to stop myself from jumping back, which was my reaction to his affectionate gesture—one that's generally reserved for dogs and very small children, preferably those who can't speak yet—because I'd thought, no doubt mistakenly, that Xenophon was wiping his greasy hand on my head. He waved me into a seat beside him. Since my arrival I'd been crouching in front of him. Not till I was seated did I catch sight of a group of followers or disciples or maybe some who were jobless or just bystanders with nothing better to do who were observing us, bathed in the mauve glow of a nearby streetlamp, quite a few girls, two or three boys, an elderly couple with a small dog and a big dog, both of them with ridiculously curly hair. Among them I recognized some individuals I'd just seen in the TV report.

"A while ago there was a drizzle, blissfully fine. I can see, Christophe, that you're suffering. Which is a good thing. We need to suffer. Suffering is the most reassuring path nowadays. Not everyone gets that chance. I'm leaving tomorrow. I can tell you. But don't tell anyone else. Also forget my old name, my old personality. They're nothing but waste. What you're looking at now is a newborn. I'm expected. A newborn is always expected. I wish I could have taken longer to grow, to enjoy my baby teeth. I have to pull them myself. Everything happens so quickly. I have a choice, of course. We all have a choice. Cowardice, stupidity, blindness, indifference, and, more than anything, selfishness, are waiting for us at the foot of our cradle. We just have to hold out a hand and take our pick. The world offers so many toys steeped in venom, in vomit, sperm, tears … "

"Xenophon, I'd like … "

"Learn how to talk, learn how to lie—they're the same thing. Learn how to make money, that's the first lesson right-minded humans consider to be essential. All other forms of learning are subordinate to that … "

"Xenophon, let me … "

"The child is decaying in his luxurious clothes, stuffed with sugar, his eyes obese. Too many images keep him from seeing the light. We must save the children from images. We must kill images, the only holy murder of our time. The child needs emptiness if he is to see the truth of space. Space is the true mother of the child. Not the mother who gives birth but the one who brings him to intelligence. Who is intelligent nowadays? A few, I grant you. But so few. It makes you shudder ... "

"Xenophon, if you knew what ... "

"Men, women, children accumulate things. That's all they do. And why do they accumulate? So they won't see their own death, won't hear the sucking insects that swirl around them constantly. Money acts like an acid that corrodes the intelligence. If each of us, for ten seconds every day, produced some intelligence, maybe hope would stop being a fairy tale for the nostalgic. But intelligence is the most painful cross to bear in our time ... "

"Xenophon, I want to tell you that ... "

"Forget my old name."

"What?"

"I'm not Xenophon any more. Call me Come-Back-to-Me."

"That sounds kind of strange."

"If I were still called Xenophon, you wouldn't have come to see me."

"Come-Back-to-Me ... "

"That's right, call me Come-Back-to-Me."

"Come-Back-to-Me, there are so many things I'd like to talk about with you. First of all, I want to explain ... "

"No, no."

"No, no what?"

"You don't have to explain anything. In fact, I've been expecting you."

"Did you know I was coming to see you?"

"Don't *you* credit me with idiotic powers. I don't work miracles, I don't predict the future. I try to see things clearly, that's all. Isn't it normal for your friend to know you, to guess why you've come?"

"But Xenophon, it's been months since we've seen each other and some incredible things have happened. If you only knew about them ... "

"The person you call Xenophon is dead."

"I'm sorry, Come-Back-to-Me. It's hard for me to ... "

"Christophe, I'm leaving tomorrow. You've come to say farewell, which is normal."

"I didn't come to ... "

"Remember how I could be silent for days? I finally understand why. Because I had nothing to say."

"A while ago, when I spotted you on TV ... "

"But now I do have something to say. I don't have the right to let my mouth sleep when the garden of the earth is being transformed into a storehouse of images. Imagine, Christophe, a painful penetration by a sword of fire. Its keen blade pierces you with no ulterior motive. It could not do otherwise. A sword of fire knows only one direction. Listen to me: I was doing the dishes when a sword of fire penetrated me. Its blazing point threw me to the floor. I howled. I was scared. I heard the cruel metal possess me. I shut myself away in the kitchen closet with the brooms and rags and garbage bags. How ignorant I was, Christophe. How young and old, but more old than young, because ensconced in my depravity, my unhealthy nonchalance, my tired hesitations, fast asleep in my own flabby person, passive, profoundly dead with my mouth open but empty, and cruel as remorse. When the sword of fire got to the end of its long journey, when it gave me back my breath, it was no longer dark in the closet. I was thinking, Christophe. I was contemplating my life, that dull lament that thought it was a song. A little light, the eye of a flashlight—that is the trace the sword of fire has left on my heart. A hole of light through which flow permanently my black thoughts, my pointless sorrows, and most of all, my fears. And as long as that shit can escape from my soul, I have enough room to let in life— real life, with its sharp rays. I am a warrior of light. I leave tomorrow to fight the images that violate children, that hypnotize the old, that disorient adults. I'm glad you came, dear Bicycle Eater. I'm glad to touch your suffering. What a fine farewell gift."

"Actually, I wanted to tell you that I went to Mexico and I was attacked by a jellyfish. The doctors can't confirm it … No, listen, I don't really know how to tell you, but I'm in the process of … "

"Aren't you going to eat the sandwich?"

"I'm not hungry."

Xenophon gathered up the bite of sandwich I'd discreetly placed on the ground, which the smaller of the two curly dogs had sniffed and then abandoned. Xenophon gobbled it, making the strange sound I'd heard earlier, a kind of *glub* that mysteriously took away from me any possibility of believing in happiness on earth.

"Christophe, I had a dream. I was walking in these enormous boots. I strode across cities, highways. I drank the rain of a storm, ate all the leaves in a forest. I was heading south. Flocks of birds, swarms of butterflies, of insects surrounded me. One day I noticed the gold of the sea on the horizon. I had reached my goal. I pulled off my boots. At once, a gigantic blue bull appeared in front of me. He was dancing on two feet, the other two held a microphone. He sang, he waddled, he drooled. Disgusting. His horns, as tall as skyscrapers, were turning on themselves, changing colour, advertising different makes of cars, projecting the distorted faces of Bogart, Hitchcock, Daffy Duck. The bull began to talk. His voice was warm. He said, 'Thank you, thank you, thank you for coming out in such large numbers.' Then he turned and with a loud noise, defecated. I was wakened by thundering applause. Okay, now I have to leave you. I've got five hundred people waiting for me in a community centre tonight. My farewell evening. Except that no one will know it. Farewell, Christophe. Don't say a word."

"What would I say?"

"That I'm leaving. No one must know."

"Why?"

"They'd try to keep me here, don't you see?"

"But where are you going?"

Into my ear. Xenophon whispered, "Hollywood." Then he took a few steps in the direction of the people who'd been watching us from the beginning. For no apparent reason he stood stock-still. It started to rain. Xenophon raised his arms to heaven, turned to me.

"Rain—this is bliss. Let it come down, Christophe, let it come down on you. I'll forget you, you forget me; but don't forget the simple bliss of the rain. Yesterday I called my mother. She said I was crazy. Insulted me. Yelled that I needed help. She thinks I was hit by lightning and it made my brain go wonky. I told her: 'Mama, I'm a newborn. Understand me. Make an effort. Mothers aren't the only ones who give birth. There is also the eternal light. I know now what path I must take. It was laid down thousands of years ago. Waiting for my footsteps. Tomorrow, I'll set them down one by one, I won't count them, it doesn't matter how many it will take. Hell is here on earth and I have to accept that. Evil doesn't fall from the sky. It is created here on earth. It is thought, planned, manufactured, mass-produced, broadcast, advertised from all the rooftops of the world. Its ugliness is dressed in fashionable garments.

Its stench is camouflaged by exorbitantly costly perfumes. Its grating voice is dubbed by stars who're paid millions to toss into the world words that are hideous, violent, polluted. Everything that's rotten, deformed, provocative, shit-eating, ah yes, shit-eating and sex-eating and money-eating—all those garbage-mouths that devour, that contaminate themselves through fornication, nowadays it's all applauded, envied, praised to the skies. The Image Machine, the Beast with a Hundred Thousand Faces, must be destroyed.' My mother wouldn't listen to me. She hung up. She didn't hear the main point."

"The main point?"

"I wanted to tell my mother that I love her. I know perfectly well what she thinks of me. There are so many lunatics in the big cities of this world, who lug around their lost children's souls, their dirty clothes, their dead eyes. I'm not that kind of ghost. The light that illuminates me is not made of illusions. My mother thinks I do drugs, just because once, when I was sixteen, she caught me with a little hash. Since then she's been living with the false impression that her son is a wreck. Which I was, most likely. Like every child that grows. Not now, though. I'm happy, Christophe. I can see clearly now. I myself am clear. I hold out my hands to you, I feel the feverishness in your wings, knotted by doubt, paralyzed by the weakness of your heart. Look at me. Who do you see? A madman? That's what you're thinking. You're just like my mother."

"No!"

"Look down."

"What?"

"Look down. Obey me. What do you see?"

"Your feet. Naked on the cold earth."

"Touch them."

I obeyed Xenophon. He was right. I thought he was crazy. And I didn't feel like contradicting him.

"Go on! Touch them."

I glanced around me. The group on the next bench was watching us. I had the impression they were waiting, motionless, for a miracle. I touched Xenophon's feet. Nothing. I touched them again. Basically, I was waiting for the earth to split open, or for rose petals to fall from the sky. I badly needed a miracle, any miracle. Given the state I was in I would have thrown myself on the most pointless, the most revolting of miracles. Even the most invisible one—on condition that it shift the weight of my existence just one millimetre.

"You haven't noticed anything?"

"No."

Xenophon lifted one foot slightly. It was practically under my nose. I noticed a dark spot on his baby toe. Then I took a closer look and realized that Xenophon no longer had a baby toe, that in its place was an infected wound. Instinctively I inspected the other foot. Same infected wound in the same place.

"What happened?"

"I cut them off. I'll cut the others. Tomorrow before dawn, I'll set off like a warrior of light. Every step I take will be an offering of pain to the road that will bring me to my destiny."

"You're talking like Christ!"

"One day we'll all talk like Him."

"But you were an atheist before!"

"Before what? Before nothing, you mean. Christophe, the Devil exists. But so does love. The most deplorable of loves, the most banal of loves, the most silent of loves, the saddest and puniest of loves is still more luminous than the desire felt for the Beast. And I'll tell you why. Because the beauty of the Beast, the greatest splendour in all Creation, is beauty stolen, one eye at a time, from the faces of men. When Evil resembled the evil on earth, the light could do its work honestly. But Evil dresses, eats, talks, walks like Good—and does all that even better. Our time is a time of confusion, of comedy. There is no more innocence, only grasping hearts, eyes nailed shut that not even compassion or pity can extract from their blindness. Kiss my wounds, Bicycle Eater!"

"You're crazy."

"Kiss them!"

This time Xenophon presented his two feet. I had the impression that if I didn't obey him, I would trigger a certain discontent in the small group of disciples who were watching us. Quickly I touched his wounds with my lips, then straightened up.

"Come-Back-to-Me, I'd like to talk to you about myself. Strange things are happening. And I'd like to talk about Anna too!"

"You're ridiculous with that theatrical love of yours. That's not what love is."

"But I love her!"

"That's what you think. Lies! Confusion! Illusion! Look at you, aren't you the Beast? You're rotting, Christophe. Your soul is unhappy in your body. Do something for it!"

"But what?"

"Hush!"

Come-Back-to-Me placed his index finger across his lips. Then smiled at me, or rather, put back his smile, the same one he'd had when I first approached him: the smile from the news report, fixed, without mystery, relentless. He turned his back on me and walked away, followed by the group that was watching for the slightest move he made. Soon I saw them disappear in the rain and the headlights of cars. My clothes were soaking wet. Come-Back-to-Me was gone, but his words hadn't moved one centimetre. I went into a restaurant, the tackiest one I could find. I sat at the counter. Asked for a coffee. The waitress came back with someone, the boss most likely, a hairy, obese man who smelled of cheap perfume. He pointed to the door. I said, "What?"

"We don't accept your kind here."

"My kind?"

"We don't want any problems."

"What problems?"

"The discussion is over. Leave or I call the cops."

I could see that despite his corpulence, he didn't dare to touch me. The waitress, hidden in a corner, was looking at me with obvious disgust. I really had become repulsive. I didn't even deserve a coffee. I left. I started to stamp my feet, to bellow: *I'm singin' in the rain!* I could have taken thousands of bloody feet and kissed them. I could even have thrown myself on the stumps. I would have devoured them. But it was too late for me. "Why, yes," I said to myself, swept away by a joyous rage. "Come-Back-to-Me is right, I'm rotten, I am the Beast, my destiny is fulfilled without me, because who am I, *I* means nothing, *I* means a bubble that bursts whenever the notion of his existence resurfaces, *I* has no more importance than a hole in the air, it's enough not to believe in the hole and it will be erased by itself, freeing the air of the nothingness that pollutes it. Why, yes," I told myself, "what a relief it is to suffer in the very act of discovering one's happiness at being nothing more than one's destiny, which is being fulfilled without our lifting a finger, or just barely, for the essential, just the essential, must be done well." I was scaring the few passers-by I encountered, I cried out to them: "Don't look at the Beast, move away!" I observed the mist escaping from my mouth, it was cold, it was blue, it carried my gaze away with it. The mystery of existence, and the satellites of stupidity and anxiety revolving around it, shrank with every step I took. The universe, even with its alleged complexity, its elusive origin, was becoming less obscure, afflicted by a hemorrhage that was gradually stripping it of its being. *Ah! Ah!* That's right, *ah! ah!* That's what I was howling to the bare trees, the yellow lawns, the cats hiding in garbage cans, the fire hydrants gleaming on their corners, the brick walls transfigured by graffiti, the display windows dreaming of their next customer; the disembowelled sky that was relieving itself onto a city chosen out of thousands, because it housed the Beast who was sending his *ah! ah!* into the brightest October night of all time!

13

Birth of a Sexual Monster

I WENT HOME THAT NIGHT convinced that I'd been entrusted with a life already lived a thousand times before so that I could live it now, cleansed of all impurities, so that I—the empty shell of me, scarcely born, brandishing the bare minimum—could bring it to a successful conclusion. Everything that was happening to me was coming from far away. Nothing was improvised. I'd thought that coincidence, or the nonchalance of my decisions, had brought me here, passing through the fog of life like a blind man, drifting to the surface of the days that my reawakenings were soiling with their moans. *Ah! Ah!* And again *ah! ah!* Why blame some poor Mexican jellyfish for my woes? What escapes through my skin, my nostrils, my scalp has nothing to do with a tropical disease that's listed as unknown. Fully dressed in my bed I was becoming aware of the radical change in the working of my brain. I could hear the metallic sound of its argument, the definitive slam of its equations. Everything tallied. The jagged wheels of my questions were tearing me to shreds. My body was being reorganized according to coordinates that left no room for doubt (new parameters! I told myself, triumphant). I was giving birth: *ah! ah!* Why yes: *ah! ah! Ah! Ah!*

How cold was that *ah! ah!* That *ah! ah!* was swallowing
Anna. That *ah! ah!* was spattering my dark room with
snow: not the room where I shut myself away as if I were
blind in both eyes to give me the illusion that I was
creating Annas out of white stolen from the dark, but the
room in my heart where I'd allowed the red bestowed by
life to fade. I just had to close my eyes and everything
would let itself be seen with the speed of truth. Why yes, I
told myself in the silence of my naked voice, you have to
be blind not to have seen that: I was being metamorphosed
into Rita! She was no longer rotting in the sand of the Isla
Mujeres cemetery, she was decomposing here, in my flesh,
forcing my cells from their lethargy, making them produce
others—rough, starving, emerging into the open air in the
form of hairs, blisters, red eyes, heavy breathing, black
nails. Now the Beast wasn't her, it was me! And very soon
it would no longer be a question of a nice little package of
inoffensive scabs, of a rough heap of features and
puffiness, of a plain and simple disfigurement of my flesh.
No! The image I saw in the mirror announced the
imminent birth of a sexual monster!

I'd have had to kiss hundreds of feet from which the toes
had been amputated, over a period of weeks, to stop the
inevitable from happening. I was going to commit crimes
to assuage my instincts. My eyes were open at last. No!
Rather, they were splitting open. Sex. Sex and nothing but.
Rita had told me so. Now it was my turn to cry: sex! There
was nothing else on the horizon of our acts. Sex. Not the
everyday sex that we see in the movies, that billboards sell
us. Not the petty, servile, wrung-out sex that comes across
so well on TV. But inordinate sex, with no ties, no face, no
mask. Sex that encompasses darkness and light, divinity
and servility. Sex composed of matter with no spiritual

content, no cosmic pretensions, no story to tell, no glorious past to be made sense of. Sex that would be cry, howl, flight. Sex that recognizes nothing, that betrays everything, that only likes sex, sex and nothing else. Because sex has nothing to say, nothing to promise, nothing to sign. Because sex that seduces doesn't dance, doesn't wiggle, doesn't sway, it only watches, darts, with no lips, no eye.

So much for the cereal diet, now I was going to consume sex and nothing but: cold, hot, pink, red—any kind at all that came along. My appetite didn't claim it possessed a discerning arsenal of taste. Just in the building where I lived, how often could I get laid? This very evening, if I simply smashed in the neighbours' door with an axe, or kicked it (I didn't own an axe), I could violate two individuals. They wouldn't be able to resist me. Afterwards, I'd go up to the next floor: another couple, older, with a dog. Then I'd come back down, go out on the street. I felt obese, powerful, as if I were giving off a planetary odour, yes, an odour that wrapped itself around reason and shrivelled it to the size of a pistachio, *ah! ah!* That's right: *ah! ah!* I would crush those stunned pistachios in my building, my neighbourhood; I'd skewer them, take off their pants, yank off their brassieres like a row of rotten teeth, that's right, tango, tango, they all want to dance a bovine tango, they're all dying to have their hearts torn out and to be free of love once and for all, ah, what a funny word: love, let's have a laugh, but basically, in the very beautiful depths that life reserves for each of us, love, right, is the greatest fraud to have emerged from the human brain, a sheep's mouth must have been transplanted into the singers who bleat those saccharine songs on the radio, where *amour* rhymes with *toujours*. But why does intelligence melt like butter in the sun as soon as love shows up with its breath mints and its little cakes of rosemary soap? Love songs distil heroin cut with shit, they clog arteries with miserable fat, with vulgar chocolate, every love song produces a thousand cases of cardiac arrest, and the people, wasted, ask for more, and the sheep bleat again and piss on them, and the people croak with their mouths consenting, ah yes, love, an open sewer that never closes, worse than an ass, all the governments in the world should organize a Summit Against Love, it's urgent, there's widespread blindness, it's contagious, am I the only one who sees the disaster, who hears love trampling the future?

Love had destroyed me. The love that Rita had kept in her heart for Alfred finally sickened her, then killed her. The love that Lâm had for me was going to put him on the road to ruin. What did that naïve boy think? That he was going to live a blissful love with a foul-smelling beast? That the story of his insane love, more monstrous than the monster that I was, would one day be told to children, in thirty-minute TV episodes, to show them that nothing is more edifying, more hygienic, than love? Ugh! Ugh! Love scratched out eyes, crammed them into gigantic earthenware jars packed with sugar. That's where this wonderful adventure ended: in the dark and in the thick syrup of stupidity.

Huddled under the covers, I was travelling. It seemed to me that I was growing a snout. I hollowed out a tunnel in my mattress and sank into it, descending through strata of unknown matter with fresh, strong odours. Desire stretched me out. I saw myself with Anna in the little blue tent in Percé. Then on the pebble beach with my bicycle. I dug some more. I spotted the stuffed jaguar from Marlin Azul that opened its mouth and released a swarm of yellow butterflies. I tossed him a hamburger. He downed it in one bite. The butterflies were bleeding. I dug some more. My mattress was transformed into a sea of sand. At the bottom I spied needles of light. I guessed what would be waiting for me if I passed to the other side. The smell of beer and urine had alerted me. I forged ahead regardless. My head emerged in the Isla Mujeres cemetery, between Andy's legs. I clutched his yellow boxers. I spread his legs, I grabbed his prick. It was limp. I pulled and I pulled, till I managed to pull it out. A woman's sex appeared, a small slit, I put a finger inside. It was blazing hot. I wanted to insert another finger, my whole hand, but the little slit contracted. She was talking to me. I didn't understand a word. I withdrew my finger. The little slit turned red, a genuine grin. I looked up to catch sight of Andy. He was drinking a Corona and smoking. I went back to the little slit, I kissed it. It said to me, "Hi, Huachi. That's very sweet of you. You've earned a candy. Here, take this!" A Honeymoon appeared between its lips. I stuffed it in my mouth. I sucked on the chocolate, swallowed the caramel. The little slit spoke again: "You're right, Huachi, love is poison. Only sex can cope. You're on the right track. Bring your face closer. I want to see it." I pressed myself against Andy's thighs. The little slit opened and I sensed it was looking at me as if it were a breath. "You're ugly, it's true. Makes me shiver. That's good. It's easy to take. You're moulting. Soon you'll lose your skin. Who knows what will appear after that? Come on, let's see what you can do." I straightened up. Asked Andy if he had any objections. "Any what?" I repeated, "Any objections." Andy didn't seem to understand. I slapped him. He didn't react. Then he fell asleep standing there. I undressed. I laid Andy down on the sand. Pulled up his knees. The little slit was still smiling. "Let's go, come!" I kissed it again. Then told myself, "That's it, now is the moment."

Then I heard the front door open. Lâm was coming home from his shoot. I threw off my duvet. Looked at the time on the alarm clock. It was much later than I'd thought. Time had flown, I had too. But into a night from which there would be no return. Lâm must run away at once or the irreparable would happen. I was sure of it: in a few seconds I was going to throw myself at him, suck out his eyes, and swallow them whole. Wasn't that what sexual monsters did?

I could make out the sound of running water: Lâm was getting ready to take a bath. I went to the kitchen: should I get a knife? Sexual monsters often need knives to carve up their victims. I needed a knife. To buck myself up, I looked at the distorted reflection of my face on the electric kettle. A face like that warranted a knife. It reminded me of a crumbling wharf with its rotten planks dangling into the water. Nothing's less secure than a dilapidated wharf. You set one foot on it and splash! So I grabbed a steak knife. On the kitchen table I saw a small cardboard box. With a sheet of paper on top. It was a letter.

Christophe,

I didn't want to wake you up. Very early tomorrow I leave for several days. We're going to finish shooting the series outside of Montreal. I'll tell you all about it when I come home. I love you. Don't worry, things will sort themselves out. I brought you some food. It's from the shoot. There was enough for an army.

Lâm

I opened the box. There was a chicken drumstick. And a chocolate éclair. Never in my life had I seen such a sad piece of chicken. As if, with its skin covered in goose pimples and curled up slightly, with its fleshy appearance and the constipated stiffness of its form, it represented a morsel of humanity forgotten by the world and gathered up in the tense expectation that it will be devoured: a little pile of defenceless meat with a tiny container of mayonnaise next to it. How tragic life can be! How it can extract from the wall of its greyness a fragment that depicts it with all its most resounding truth! Wasn't Lâm also a piece of chicken that I was about to chew on? Of course he was. From now on, there was no more flesh, only meat. But how can an inexperienced sexual monster like me do it? I swallowed the chocolate éclair. Got whipped cream on my face and hands. I wiped them with a rag. I picked up the steak knife again and made my way to the bathroom door, stealthy as a wolf, which made sense, I *was* a wolf, a virgin, dismantled, forever lost without the shaft of the knife that was guiding me. I had the impression that I was sniffing Lâm, the amber smell of his body, through the door. I pressed my ear against it, heard a slight lapping—then nothing.

Okay, Christophe, think: you're going to open the door, and then—then what? What are you going to do? I realized it's no easy matter, being a sexual monster. There must exist a way of proceeding that would give the demented deed all its power and all its authenticity. Anna slap, help me! You'd know how to do it. You wouldn't hesitate for a second. You know the instructions both for suffering and for sensual bliss. What to do first? Kill? Love? Or love, kill? Kill? But why kill? I can cause suffering without killing. No: impossible. A sexual monster knows no half-measures. I'm in the process of committing a grave error: thinking. A sexual monster doesn't think. Charge! Yes, it's clear, I open the door and I do it. The knife. That's it. That says it all: the knife. *It* knows. Open it. Act.

Slowly I pulled the door open a crack. Lâm was asleep in the tub. He'd practically disappeared in the foam. Only his head and one foot emerged from the cloak of bubbles. His face wore a sketch of a smile, as if his smile were sleeping too. I approached. Then I saw blood on the floor tiles. Good God! Lâm's not asleep, he's dead—already! The absurd notion that I'd killed him during a mental blank petrified me. But then I was reassured. The blood was coming from me. From my thigh. I'd slashed myself with the knife without realizing. A move that had escaped me. A move of impatience, most likely. Or a nervous tic. I knelt. I gazed at Lâm's foot. It was asleep too. A dark fruit. Warm. Poised on the curved enamel of the tub. I brushed it with my lips. Tasted it with the tip of my tongue. Lâm half-opened his eyes. At once our gazes burned, together. I stood up, made my getaway. I slipped on the blood. Got up again, left the apartment, disappeared into the night.

What kind of monster was I? I hid in a backyard. I was shaking. Trying to get my breath back. I still held the steak knife. I raised my arm and threw it. It was raining. I was shivering. My leg was bleeding. Pain, late, had caught up with me in the cold, the mud. At dawn I could finally close my eyes. When I opened them again four little girls were looking at me. They had on happy coats, multicoloured school bags, and flowery umbrellas. I moved my numb, injured leg. At once they fled, horrified, emitting high-pitched shrieks. My wounds had stopped bleeding. I limped in the direction of Saint-Louis Square. My clothes were wet. I shouted, "Don't go yet, Come-Back-to-Me, I'm going with you! Save me! Save me!" I circled the park several times, shouting. No sign of Come-Back-to-Me. I sat on a bench. Looked at the people crossing the park. They seemed so well-adjusted to life. They all had a goal, bags, eyes, boots, watches, appointments. I sat for hours, motionless as a pile of stones. I was emptying myself, no rush. No one disturbed me. No one sat beside me. No one. I was no longer part of this world. I went home.

The little cardboard box was still on the kitchen table, but with a new sheet of paper on top. Another letter from Lâm. Longer than the previous one. He wrote that he'd waited till the last minute but he'd absolutely had to leave and join the film crew. My behaviour in the bathroom had disconcerted him. He'd cleaned up the blood. He'd thought I'd hurt myself by slipping while I was running. I concluded that he hadn't noticed the steak knife. Yet he claimed to be happy. "Never," he wrote, "has a kiss brought me such a feeling of lightness and fire." He talked about the future. He hoped for the impossible. He also talked about Anna. Assured me that I would recover. One of the technicians had told him that his cousin's boyfriend had been in Mexico and when he came home, his skin had been covered with scabs. He'd thought he was going to die. The doctors had finally discovered that he suffered from impetigo, a minor little condition marked by pustules that a simple anti-something cream would burst and then dry up. The guy couldn't wait to go back. He insisted, "Call me as soon as you can!" He gave me a phone number and the name of an inn at Percé. The final sequence of *Cul-de-sac II* was going to be shot there. The scriptwriter and the director had insisted on setting the final episode in a romantic locale familiar to the general public. The heroic couple, Isabelle and Tâm, would finally—after a thousand incredible adventures—experience the ecstasy of physical love against the background of the Percé Rock and the sea glittering under the moon's white eye. Clichés, every one, but certainly an unforgettable ending for *Cul-de-sac II*—an apotheosis, wrote Lâm, that could lead to *Cul-de-sac III*.

I opened the box and consumed the drumstick. I sat in the living room, facing the window that looked out on Coloniale Avenue. Night fell. Outside, rain and wind. Turbulent branches were scratching at the window. I opened wide the curtains. On the wet streets I could see monsters walking around in groups. And then I realized that one year before, to the day, I had stolen Anna's coat. It was Halloween. Like tonight. But tacky monsters didn't scare me now. They had not encountered the blinding nature of the genuine living dead. I'd doused all the lights in the apartment except for one little candle that I didn't take my eyes off of. It was now my soul, that tiny bit of fire that had trouble staying upright on its cliff of wax. Soul of nothing because good for nothing. Oh! The wind! The wind! How vicious it was that night. Demented! Why was it howling like a sad wolf? I cried out to it, "Don't stop howling, it warms me."

My thoughts were flowing like a transparent stream. Something inside me no longer wanted to be a man, just a shadow, a floating apparition with no strings, no pretensions.

Therefore I do not exist. The sound of night passes through me. I am born. That's it. The night has one more flaw. Somewhere, someone is always waiting for a newborn. Here I come. My footsteps are sleazy. I cross streets swept clean by life, I'd thought to bring along an apple, an old one I found in the fridge, I'll save it for later, do something for your soul, okay, fine, whatever it wants, I'm in luck, I'm suffering, others die of pleasure, look, I've just given my apple to a child in a Yogi the Bear costume, the city is blue and lustrous, I devour the brick walls, the asphalt, the broken cement of the sidewalks, the last autumn leaves, shreds, soon transformed into dust, their smell radiates to my bronchial tubes, why yes, of course, life has too many senses, some have to be cut, keep just a few, the ones you can hold in your hand, the ones that, without the slightest effort, you can drop to the ground as if they were an empty package of gum, I turned left here, now I just have to go back up to Saint-Joseph Boulevard, that's a road I could travel with my eyes shut, it's already been a year since I've dragged my feet up here, I've changed, just watch me for a while, you'll see I'm not the same, let me hold you tight in my arms, I've been thinking about you for a while now, I need to press my face against your rough bark, to smell your odour of wet wood, if anyone knows my illusions, it's you, Fred, you and no one else, you're my tree, I'm your man, we've never been in any kind of trouble, without you I'd have long ago jumped out the window, that one, just above your top branches, the one I've opened dozens of times to talk about Anna in secret, I would arrive from her bedroom where I'd spend hours watching her sleep, I'd straighten up, hardly breathing, after bending over her in her sleep, I'd wonder how fragile Anna's eyelids were, I'd exclaim in silence, like a fish swallowing air, about the sacred office of those two small pieces of flesh that divided the universe in two, that expelled me to the other end of the planet Anna, that transformed me into a tightrope-walker condemned to spend his life on the high wire of hope, whose end was so far away, it made us assume that it didn't exist, how many times had I nearly wakened Anna with a kiss, hopeful that the opening of her eyelids would be followed by the opening of her arms, never, Fred, never have I had the courage to do it, KO'ed, I went back to the living room, opened the window, and bothered you with my pissing and moaning, but you've always listened to me with that mystery of yours amplified by the wind, you never rejected my words, you mixed them in with the rustling of your leaves, you're my friend, I don't need to take a knife and carve in your bark *Christophe loves Fred* and enclose it in a heart, you've always known that you and me, it was for life, okay, kiss-kiss, I need to feel your big chunk of life, so upright and steady, I'm going now, that's it, I'm not here any more, I am there, did I dream, didn't Fred tell me when I left him that I was pathetic, yes, he even repeated it, that's the only thing he can say in any case, it's not his fault, he's a pathetic-tree, a sage, he knows perfectly well that the same words, perpetually repeated, are all it takes to exhaust any meaning, to express everything that matter can spew as stories to entertain men and their offspring, so yes, I'm pathetic, I come forward anyway, I empty my pockets of all the money I could find at home, I ask, is that enough, that's enough, replies the man behind the glass in his ticket office, I've got an hour's wait, I wait for an hour, I pile onto the bus for Percé, seventeen hours later I get off, it's afternoon, the sun is out, it's cold, the air is brisk, the wind is savage, as if there were metal in the air, I down two coffees, I don't have enough money for a sandwich, I can hear conversations around the counter where I've taken a teaspoon to scrape up the sugar at the bottom of my cup, people are talking about the filming of *Cul-de-sac II*, the technicians are getting ready to shoot on the beach, the stars have flown in, they'll be filming tonight, I go out, make my way to the wharf, spot a cluster of bystanders watching the preparations, excited children run around, women laugh, a man smokes a pipe, there are trailers parked along the side of the road, I'm sure that Anna and Lâm are in one of them—unless each of them has his own—the youngsters try to get closer but the guards shoo them away, I have the impression that the 4,000 residents of Percé have dropped their usual occupations and turned their attention to *Cul-de-sac II*, I look at the sea, which is turning darker in the distance, in the sky I spot flocks of birds, white smudges circling, I hear bells, I turn around, I see people going into a church, I join them, and would you look at that, I'm attending a Mass or a service, I don't know, there are lots of elderly people, the priest raises his arms, someone plays the organ, the priest tells a story, repeating frequently, "My dear brethren," he says that today we are celebrating with jubilation All Saints' Day, the feast day of every saint, "every saint," he repeats again, I look around me, people stand, sit, kneel, the scent of incense is in the air, I'm allergic to incense, never mind, the priest invites the faithful to come back the following day, "Don't forget," he says, "tomorrow, November 2, is the Day of the Dead, all of you, dear brothers and sisters, have a dead person, two, three, several dead persons who need you, do not forget them tomorrow, respect their memories, pray for their souls, just one day a year, that's not much to ask of you, the living, you have the other 364 days, so, how about it, tomorrow, don't just light a candle, light up your heart as well," now people are leaving the church, several have already left, anxious to go back and watch the preparations for *Cul-de-sac II*, I stay there by myself, I wait, the priest comes back, approaches me, asks me to leave, he's going to lock the church, I leave, it's already dark, I spot the priest, he's also making his way towards the filming, I lose sight of him in the crowd, people in fluorescent orange sweats push the crowd away, "please, step back, there's nothing to see, let us do our jobs," I hear rumours, someone saw one of the actors, who's even more gorgeous in person; they should be here soon, several hours go by, many people have left, discouraged, annoyed, frozen, they didn't see the stars who are cozy and warm in their trailers, the director is quite clear, the scene won't be shot as long as clouds are hiding the moon, he needs the full moon in all its grandeur, they haven't travelled thousands of kilometres to film without the main character, technicians grumble, everyone's guzzling coffee, partaking of sandwiches, I've managed to grab a few for myself, most of the people are looking up at the sky, waiting for moonbeams to break through, behind me I hear a whisper, I turn around, a woman in her forties with a red nose, is praying, "Hail Mary full of grace ... " a young man with red-rimmed glasses, an assistant most likely, goes up to the director, says something into his ear, the director pushes him away violently, stamps his feet, "no way will I have a virtual moon cut in, it's the final scene of the series, the audience is entitled to a real one," I spot Anna, she has a blanket around her shoulders, I don't want her to see me, I hear her complain, voices are raised, all kinds of people are talking at once, arguing, crying, howling, some applaud, everyone looks up at the sky, the moon has just punched a hole in the night, the wind comes up, a squall lasting several seconds, then all is calm and they clear the decks for action, "Hurry up, move it, in your places, come on, come on, move your butts," real emotion runs through the small group who've braved the cold and endured the wait, the woman who was praying offers me some cherry gum, I take it, but I'm ashamed when I feel her eyes on my face, the people in fluorescent orange push us back and clear a large perimeter in front of the stage, Lâm is already in position, a blanket over his shoulders, he's standing close to Anna, they aren't looking at one another, they look like two victims of a highway accident, someone lights the campfire that have been built near a tent, a woman in an anorak pours champagne into glasses and arranges them amid the remains of a meal scattered over a tablecloth on the ground, the spots are lit, a makeup-person touches up the faces of Anna and Lâm, in a few moments the set comes to life, an idyllic scene already filmed a thousand times, a handsome young couple who've overcome the forces of evil, are about to merge in this magical setting—the sea, the moon, the campfire, a frugal repast with plenty to drink and the mysterious mass that draws one's eyes—the Percé Rock—a dark presence grazed by the flight of gulls, sacred opening that will legitimize the union of our heroes, the director goes up to his stars, whispers something, someone takes their blankets, two butterflies extricate themselves from their cocoons, everyone is stunned, the beauty of Anna, the beauty of Lâm are stunning, no doubt about it, space pulls away from the edges of the world and gathers around them, gratifying them with an overabundance of white, with a luxurious contour, with volatile pigmentation—all that at once, as if their bodies could be both in spots dense and porous, both touchable and untouchable, no one speaks, everyone is looking, absorbing, punch-drunk, yes, punch-drunk from the beauty quivering before them, Anna has on a light, flaky dress, Lâm is in overalls without a shirt, I see them shivering from the cold, I wait for the director to shout "Action!" everyone has turned towards him, but he gestures without opening his mouth, rolling, Anna and Lâm stop shivering, their eyes light up, summer has just arrived, their summer, Isabelle and Tâm are dancing, the moon sparkles, very professionally she has slipped inside the frame, to the place recommended by the age-old laws of love, it is the eye that says yes, unable to close, giving the flesh no respite, the director of *Cul-de-sac I* and *II* and all the other *Cul-de-sac*s to come—countless, no doubt—is a genius, I admit it, he's correct right down the line, not one so-called "artistic" photo is anywhere near as good as what he's shooting now, Tâm drops a kiss on Isabelle's shoulder, their silent dance goes blurry, they head for the campfire, they've picked up glasses of champagne along the way, they turn towards the Percé Rock and gaze at it, locked together, they sit, drain their glasses, the camera, on a dolly, is coming towards them, wedges them between the landscape and its glass and metal paraphernalia, I can't see them now, I move, walk around the set, near them is a man holding a long mike boom, Isabelle bows her head, Tâm drops the straps of his overalls, his slim, sculpted torso emerges in the play of fleeting shadows projected by the campfire, Tâm slips his hand under Isabelle's dress, she arches her back, her nipples are visible under the fabric of her dress, Tâm is licking them as if he were a little cat, they kiss, the director shouts "Cut!" and Isabelle and Tâm kiss again, even more passionately, "Cut! Cut!", the makeup person and her assistant with the red glasses separate the actors, the director goes up to them, "That was perfect, gave me goosebumps, but you were acting as if we were in the next scene, the one by the campfire should be more restrained, kisses, sure, caresses, no problem, all that's perfect but don't forget, there still has to be a bit of awkwardness, not a lot, just a hint, enough to boost the desire for the scene in the tent, and above all, don't forget the confessions, that's what matters here, the confessions, okay, let's go back to the kissing scene, but with some awkwardness, okay, a little clumsiness too, then continue with the script, but you were fabulous, I can sense that you're in love, it's powerful, it comes across, oh wow, it really comes across, okay now, let's get moving, Lady Moon may be on her way out, put the props back, quick-quick, yes, yes, pour a little champagne into the glasses, and throw a log on the fire," I look up, the moon is still there, he's right, they're in love, oh yes, it comes across, it comes across to me all right, the camera is rolling again, they finish their champagne, I sense the discomfort, my discomfort that cuts right through me, yes, we delegate some strange machines to you, to pick up a little more of your beauty, but we are nothing, nothing but insects that live for just one night and are found burned to cinders in the morning, I stare at them hungrily again, it doesn't much matter if it's Anna or Isabelle, Lâm or Tâm—those names melt like sugar in the bodies they think they're crowning with their syllables, I'm no longer a mouth for Anna, I won't repeat that name which has burned my lips, I watch Lâm slip his hand under Anna's dress, he does it awkwardly, actors are so obedient, if the director had asked Lâm to strangle Anna he'd have done it, but he asked him to love her, clumsily, so now he doesn't know how to caress her, and Anna no longer offers her mouth with such abandon, Lâm lowers his head, speaks, says, "Isabelle, there's something I want to tell you, I was lying before, I've never had a girlfriend and I'm not what you think, you're … you are the first woman in my life, you're a virgin, Tâm, yes, that's wonderful, me too, you too Isabelle, yes, my love, I've also lied to you, you're the first man in my life, it's wonderful," together, they repeat "It's wonderful," they get up, head for the tent, "Cut!" everyone applauds, "Set up the lights for the tent scene," blankets and coffee are brought for Anna and Lâm, who step aside, grips take over the set, shift equipment, I look at the moon, I look at the Percé Rock, my hand is inside my coat, on the handle of a knife, Anna and Lâm step inside the tent, a floodlight comes on inside, their silhouettes appear, the director repeats his magic gesture, the camera is rolling, the shadows of Anna and Lâm ripple on the canvas of the tent, they embrace, merge, are drowned in one another, overwhelmed, then separate, the silhouettes appear again, we hear music, I recognize it from the first note, "Let's Call the Whole Thing Off," oh,

Anna, why, why did you do that, our song, you gave it to the director of *Cul-de-sac*, you're heartless, my little love, what is it that's moving about in your chest, a bird with no memory, an empty drawer, oh, I'm sorry, Anna, I'm sorry, I have no right now to use your name as if it were the most ordinary thing, available to anyone at all, I give you back your two sacred syllables, I can't find fault with anything about you, who am I to do such a thing, dance, Anna, dance with Lâm, "you like potatoes and I like potahtoes," yes, dance, aren't you two nothing but shadows gripped by desire, aren't you made of matter that rises with the moon, that unravels with time, vague matter, yes, who's who, who takes off whose dress, who uncovers the curve of whose ass, who sways in the flight of insects shredded by the light, "you like tomatoes," the moon also "likes tomatoes," red, round, full, stuck in the corner of the frame like a smear of glitter, there they are, they're naked but we can see nothing, and it's alarming, that nothing in their flesh, that eye that never makes free with their flesh, that eye, my eye, the eyes of millions of viewers, the camera's eye, the director of *Cul-de-sac* is a genius, to place two lovers in a tent, put the lights inside, and make a show of the convulsion of their sexual shadow, of their spasm on a night when the moon is full with, as a bonus, the hole in the Percé Rock, one-eyed big cat licked by the dying tide, "let's call the whole thing off," this is it, they're doing it inside that blue tent which has imprisoned my dream, they're doing it, the word *love* no longer makes me want to laugh, to mock, the word *love* being made before my eyes stops being a word, Anna's hair explodes, Lâm's hips are disconnected, I approach, the shadows throb against the canvas, multiplied, I see a tiger, he opens his mouth, his mouth is twisted, it's a hot-air balloon, a parasol, an eagle that cleaves the air, crashes, is reborn in the form of a dolphin, it swells, splits in two, hesitates, is recast as a succulent plant that flutters, spurts, is scattered in wavelets, I close my eyes, I take a step, I look again, love has nothing to do with me and I have nothing to do with love, the director is about to exclaim, "Cut!" I run towards the light, I plant the knife in the canvas of the tent, now instead of rushing, time flows like syrup, congeals, I'm caught inside it, I look at Anna and Lâm, naked, some unique thing, a sweating thing that questions me, cries out with its eyes, the light from the floodlights burns me, I draw a blank, why have I come to Percé, I look in the eyes of Anna and of Lâm for the answer, ah yes, the knife, yes, the knife ... the Night of the Butterflies, I know now what happened down there ... the urge to kill ... yes, I brought my arm up, I aimed at Rita's heart, I closed my eyes ... I brought the knife down with a cry ... if Rita hadn't pulled away at the last second, I would have killed her ... I am ... a monster ... that's why I have a knife in my hand, has time started moving again, no, not yet, time is sitting in a corner and watching, what are all those people doing behind me, crying out, I kneel, no, I bow my head, but it's the same thing, the director repeats "Cut! Cut!", time starts moving again, I straighten up, I bring down my arm, I plant the knife in the other wall of the tent, I run away through the opening, knocking over some lights, I hear an explosion, I turn around, I spy Anna and Lâm emerging from the flaming tent, they're safe, people are stamping on the tent to keep the fire from spreading, I run straight ahead, my feet sink into the mud, suddenly the sky swallows the moon, and the night swallows the sky, in the distance I can make out the disturbing mass of the Percé Rock, I hear my name, Lâm is shouting it, I move on without catching my breath, I can't see anything now, the low tide has left puddles, slippery pebbles, waterlogged seaweed, what else, oh yes, thousands of corpses no doubt, infected wrecks, neglected keepsakes, leftover hearts, waste matter of love, I can't see them but I trample them with every step, in this place, at this time, everything is shaped like a rat—slimy, sad, split in two, the wind comes up again, is it the wind, no, it's a howl, I can hardly breathe, I advance, advance, the ocean fills me with its roaring, I sink to my knees in something soft, a rat split in two, what else in this place in the world, I extricate myself, start running again, fall, my mouth is full of mud, I struggle, I advance on all fours, my knees are bleeding, where is the knife, I don't have it any more, I look for it in the darkness, I give up, I am made of what, of sea wrack, that's certain, I am the man with thighs of clay, fish-thighs, I go *ah! ah!* A newborn goes *ah! ah!* to the people bending over him, it's my turn to go *ah! ah!* to the universe that's milling beneath me, *ah! ah!* to the Percé Rock, which sends me its breath of sediment and gull droppings, *ah! ah!* to the little flower of fate ... ah, the moon, she resurfaces, ah, she's even fuller than a while ago, as if she has devoured the clouds that were choking her, the moon over the Percé Rock is a thousand times fuller than the one above Isla Mujeres, a thousand times more intelligent, a thousand times older, a thousand times more indifferent, it's just a hole in my memory, I arrive at the Rock like an animal, grey, with split ends, I stand up, I am holding a flat stone, I spy some white spots on the walls of the Rock, maybe some birds that have forgotten to fly south, or are they souls that have built their nests in the rock out of stubbornness, yes, they're souls, I can hear them wheeze, I'm not cold any more, I'm not anything, all I have is the flat stone and my mud-soaked clothes, I walk towards the hole in the Rock, I stand in the middle, the sound of the ocean rushes inside, I'm going to do something for my soul, I'm going to free it from the Beast,

Rita, it's your feast day, the priest said so a while ago, it's midnight now, happy Day of the Dead, but stay dead, above all, stay dead, let me bid farewell to the love that isn't made, farewell to all the copulations dreamed of a thousand times over, farewell to all the ghost kisses that wander in search of the beloved face, farewell to the orphan caresses, farewell to penetrations that have penetrated nothing but the wind, farewell to the damp words that have never been dropped into an ear, it's still midnight, the moon slips her eye into the hole in the Rock, the night is turning white, I am the man of mud and sea wrack, my thigh-fish are tearing their muscles and swallowing sea spray, I don't have impetigo, the blood of the jellyfish flows in my veins, a happy fish that intoxicates me, I understand why midnight is not advancing, it's waiting for me, the knife—it wasn't for Anna and Lâm, but for me, I know that now, I drop my pants, I sit in the centre of the hole, in front of me chance has placed a stone, chance or fate, something has deposited before me a stone, a piece of limestone fallen off the Rock, I sit in front of it, I've lost the knife but I have the stone, I take my cock in my left hand, I stretch it, I tell myself that if I had ten cocks I'd crush them all, I look up, a flock of gulls free themselves from the Rock and come down towards me, before they get here I raise my right hand very high and I smash the stone onto my cock.

14

Sleeping Cutie

ONE YEAR LATER, on November 2, the Day of the Dead, I come back to myself in a hospital room. By losing my virginity to Anna. Lâm held in his arms a little girl named Lili.

Lâm and Anna give me the details. That night, the entire crew and some of Percé's inhabitants had gone looking for me. They found my body just in time: before the rising tide could wash it out of the hole in the rock and carry it out to sea. I had lapsed into a deep coma. A small plane brought me back to Montreal. My parents were summoned to my bedside at once. They'd just inherited a vegetable. The doctors had doomed me, though they couldn't explain why I'd gone into a coma. I had experienced a shock, a small one, which explained nothing. I hadn't crushed my cock with the stone. When my saviours found me, it was my thumb that was smashed to a pulp. My aim had been off.

The director of *Cul-de-sac* had thought my forced entry into the tent brilliant. It had inspired him. He'd re-shot the scene. In the new version, Isabelle and Tâm did not experience the first ecstasy of physical love. A maniac armed with a gigantic pair of pruning shears was slashing the tent to shreds. After a chase and a battle filled with startlingly athletic pirouettes, our heroes had managed to deliver the maniac back to the world of psychiatry and prison. The viewer had no choice but to wait for *Cul-de-sac III* to witness the conclusion of the young couple's lovemaking. But Anna was pregnant. The script for *Cul-de-sac III* had been entirely reworked around the character of the likable young go-getter Tâm and his adventures, with Anna required for just a few appearances: medium shots that showed her from her breasts up, and close-ups of her face. *Cul-de-sac IV* would finally consecrate the love of the two adventurers in a scene that was being publicized as the most daring, the most erotic in the history of television. An audience survey had shown that Anna's recent motherhood did not endanger in the least the credibility of her character who because of circumstances had remained a virgin. The audience loved Anna. The audience loved her baby. The audience loved Lâm, the papa. The audience adored all three and they wanted more.

On the Day of the Dead that entire holy family had ended up in my room. I was a handsome sight. A prince. A sleeping cutie, as Lâm had dubbed me. The coma had been the most successful remedy for all my physical woes. My skin had shed its scabs and pustules. I no longer resembled an alligator. Nothing seemed to torment me now. Anna of the two sacred syllables had lain down on me and given me a kiss. She had stayed there on my body, crying, while Lâm gazed at us, with little Lili in his arms. The touch of her tears on my cheeks had suddenly extricated me from my lethargy. With no transition, I'd come back to what is naïvely known as "myself." Small spasm of a blue bulb.

I couldn't make the slightest move though, not even to open my eyes. I didn't know where I was or why. For a moment I was just one thing: the awareness of Anna's tears on my face. And that was all. A mirror that collects a warm liquid. My instinct for life, wrapped around a tear, was absorbing its most microscopic elements. It analyzed, regrouped, reorganized, and identified them: Anna. Anna was the one crying over me. But why? She'd planted another kiss on my lips which as a result were born onto my amorphous face. Then she'd got up again and I'd had the sensation that she had taken with her my skin, that she'd pulled it off me, welded it to hers, that I was lying there not naked but flayed, on what I now figured to be a bed. Mine? Surely not. Next, my sense of smell was wakened. No doubt about it: I was not at home. It smelled of hospital. Then I heard voices. They unravelled like a piece of cloth that's being torn. I managed now and then to save an intact word from that jumble. Little by little, the puzzle of my existence was being put back together. I had of course recognized Anna's voice, but I'd also recognized Lâm's. They were talking about me. In slow motion. I was finding it rather hard to follow them. When I finally understood what they were saying, I let out a cry. A gigantic howl. Anna and Lâm went on talking. Kept repeating the same thing: "His parents have made their decision: twelve months of anguish, of thwarted hopes, they're resigned, we have to see it from their point of view, look at him, he's found something, he's carefree, at peace, his face is radiant, he was in torment, every breath demanded an effort of the imagination, but he's still breathing, it's not him breathing, it's his lungs, he isn't even there any more, you understand, yes, but it's hard, his parents made the right decision, I would have done the same thing, anyone would have done the same thing, no, I don't agree, I would have waited a while longer, stop, you're making yourself sick, imagine being in his position, he's sunk in black concrete, he may be in agony, who knows, no, no way, the doctors are absolutely sure, he doesn't feel anything, he's clinically dead, doctors, doctors, what do they know, they're human beings like us, they make mistakes like anyone else, more often, even because their profession puts them in situations where only mystery is holding up its end, you're right, but you have to agree, it can't go on like this, tonight they're going to pull the plug, poor Christophe … "

Pull the plug? I panicked when I realized that I was imprisoned in my body, that wires, tubes, and probes were connecting me to the world, that one click would wipe out this imitation of a life, that in a few hours' time and with my parents' authorization, a stranger in a white coat—I can even smell the starch—was going to pull the plug, that I would depart to drift forever, eyes open under paralyzed eyelids. I tried again to cry out but only I could hear the roar of my despair. On the surface of my body, nothing had moved. A lake from which the wind had been driven away. It was harder and harder to hear the voices of Anna and Lâm. Were they leaving the room? If I too could cry, produce a tear, just one, maybe someone would see it glittering in the corner of my eye, maybe someone would realize that there was still a little light on somewhere inside me. How to produce a drop of water when one is only blackness and immobility? I was lost in my body. It could begin kilometres away from me. Where inside me was the place where it would flow?

In a final effort, I gathered together everything I had been—memories, hopes, desires, remorse, fears, dreams, lies, vanity, hypocrisy, passion, appetite, humiliation, vengeance, bitterness, love, laughter—all that I mixed together in the hope that it would become a tear that would answer the one that Anna had dropped onto my cheek by way of farewell a few moments ago. I pushed, pushed. Suddenly I felt something. A loosening. An opening. A flash. A lightning flash. Yes, something had finally stirred inside my body. The rest happened very fast. My body had given birth not to a tear, but to an erection. It was my cock on which my cry had been concentrated. Lâm, before he left the room, had turned around to look at me one last time. He'd taken a step towards my bed. He thought he saw my sheet rise up. Having convinced himself that he'd been dreaming, he was going back to Anna when my sheet started to quiver again. He rushed to me, threw back my sheet. His warm hand made me open my eyes. They were dry, clear. I looked at Lâm. Without words, I spoke to him. Without hearing, he listened. I could see in his eyes that he'd understood me. He left the room, came back a few moments later with Anna.

Then Anna offered me her body. Mine came back into the world at the moment it experienced, for the first time, an orgasm.

Anna.

15

Come-Back-to-Me

A FEW WEEKS LATER I WAS WALKING, I was getting dressed by myself.

Shortly before my release from the hospital, expected to be around Christmas, I'd had a TV set installed in my room. Anna and Lâm had promised to come and watch with me "The Making of *Cul-de-sac*"—a special on the new series that would run in the spring. It would show the filming, Anna and Lâm in their new house with their baby, and even—a first—excerpts from the scene that the entire population was waiting to see so they could participate, in their own way, in the carnal union of Isabelle and Tâm. On the night of the telecast, I was waiting impatiently for the arrival of Anna and Lâm, each of whose visits created waves of excitement in the hospital staff. In fact I think that thanks to my famous visitors, I'd become a patient they were proud to be caring for. I switched on the TV in advance. Zapping, I stumbled on Xenophon.

A Montreal TV crew had gone to Los Angeles to film a story on the Come-Back-to-Me phenomenon. In just one year, he'd become a religious star and the American talk shows were fighting over him. Crowds came to hear him at shopping malls on the main streets. His hair was even longer, his beard even more historic, his eyes even more hollow. He preached a return to the original values of the

Christ child—before the church took him over—
denounced the twelve apostles, called them "twelve
traitors," warned humankind about the omnipotence of
the Devil, declared that the holy war had started, spat on
the cameras that were filming him, spread his arms, and
explained his loathing of the children of America—most of
them rotten and carriers of germs—then shrieked that the
others—the pure, the naïve, the rare ones not yet bitten by
the bitch that was money, sex, playthings, fashion, drugs,
those not yet hypnotized by Hollywood and its herd of
golden calves, its starlets with the lewd organs, its
brainwashed cowboys good for nothing but driving jeeps
and squeezing triggers—must be saved. This time the
camera couldn't zoom in on Xenophon's feet: they no
longer existed.

Xenophon had kept his promise. He'd even gone further:
he had cut off his toes and his feet. Both legs ended in
stumps. Come-Back-to-Me got around only by wheelchair,
which a bunch of carefully-dressed disciples quarrelled over
for the honour of pushing it. In a more serious tone, the
reporter told viewers that the new prophet's amputated
parts had become lucrative objects on the black market.
False disciples were selling relics of Come-Back-to-Me. A
toe could go for as much as ten thousand dollars. These
relics, false or genuine—but surely false, most of them,
because a quick investigation already showed upwards of a
hundred fervent toe-owners, not counting those who
announced their intention to buy a little piece of heel or any
other part of the foot—were considered to have healing
powers. Come-Back-to-Me had even declared that he was
going to cut off his legs and after that, the rest, all the rest,
that he would thereby go up step by step to heaven—which
was the least he could do in the name of Love. The reporter
then announced a scoop: Come-Back-to-Me had promised

a major U.S. network that he would cut off his right stump, live, in their studio, on Christmas night. He had mentioned that he'd slice off as much as ten centimetres of flesh. As had the earlier report, this one ended on a close-up of the face of the new prophet who, with a very pronounced French accent, seemed to be speaking only to me: *I am who I am, I am Come-Back-to-Me.*

I turned off the TV, disgusted. Looked at my smashed thumb. A good-sized chunk of it was missing. Basically, I was just as bad as Xenophon. We were both monsters. But he, this Come-Back-to-Me, had found his god: showbiz. His grotesque sacrifice reached its apogee before the greedy gaze of TV studios. And me? I had found nothing but failure. I was a monster of incapacity, blindness, passivity. What insipid sacrifice had I offered to the eyes of the world? A piece of thumb. I'd been incompetent from start to finish. I'd screwed up everything. I'd had to fall into a coma in order to make love for the first time in my life. I was nearly thirty years old. And now? Now I was waiting in a hospital room, waiting for Anna and Lâm. But what did I expect from them? Even more, what could I offer them? I was even jealous of Lili who condensed, in the small space she occupied in the world, the tremendous beauty of both her parents. They were three, happy and complete. What was I doing in their lives? *I am who I am.* But who exactly am I?

It was decided: I wouldn't watch the "making of" *Cul-de-sac IV*. If I still possessed a little will, a little heart, I had to forget Anna and Lâm, step out of their lives, never see them again. I doffed my PJs, donned jeans, sweater, coat. And fled.

I had thought that making a getaway from a hospital wouldn't be easy. But I'd simply had to behave normally and I was able to pass quite easily through the main glass door that opened onto the sidewalk. After all, didn't I look normal? I was greeted by the stinging cold. I stuffed my hands into my coat pockets and walked.

To walk, to move away, to disappear. To be alone with one's footsteps, with the street, with the neon lights of the city that the December cold kept in a sort of stupor. Snow was falling. It was perhaps winter's first.

16

Fred

SOME YEARS LATER, Anna killed herself during the shooting of a film. Initially, millions of admirers wouldn't believe the story about a defective parachute as reported by all the media, interrupting normal programming. But finally they accepted it. I'd believed it right away. My heart had hurt too much. Anna hadn't wanted a stunt woman to stand in for her.

Like thousands of others, I waited outside the church for the main doors to open and let Anna's coffin pass through, followed by a long funeral procession of sad people. That was when I saw Lâm. He was holding the hand of a little girl of six. There was spontaneous applause when the coffin passed: a final tribute to Anna. I felt a pang of anguish. I watched Lâm move away. I hadn't been able to get his attention.

Shortly afterwards, the city was hit by an ice storm. At dawn, I rushed outside and gazed, fascinated, at building fronts, cars, garbage cans. A supernatural harmony linked all those objects. A heavenly painter had made of Montreal a picture in which beauty, without sleeping, reached the perfection of stillness. I was no longer strolling in a city but in the dream it had invented for itself without asking the inhabitants' permission. Like a child astronaut I slipped between the rifts in a harsh and stubborn landscape.

In Saint-Louis Square a branch fell from a tree. I narrowly managed to avoid it. Then, very quickly, other branches couldn't resist the weight of the accumulated ice. Fred! I thought about him right away. I raced as fast as I could to Saint-Joseph Boulevard. Fred was lying across the street, broken inside his glassy suit. Some people were yelling at others to go home. The city was becoming dangerous. Fred had crushed a car. I approached and put my bare hands on him. The ice melted under my palms. I stuck my ear against his trunk: I could detect a slight dark tingling. An insistence on stretching out further in time. I embraced the tree of my secrets with arms that were too short. I tried to melt into him. I was crying but didn't realize it. Crying over Anna's death. My body sank slowly into the bark of the tree. I disappeared. Suddenly I was floating inside Fred. It was white, blinding—then restful. The tree was flowing like a river. I set out with it. The current carried me very far. I cried out, "Fred, where are you taking me?" He replied without further ado, "To the land of four letters!" What was he talking about? I cried, "What are you talking about, Fred?" He laughed, then repeated, "One, two, three, four, one two, three four … "

"But Fred, I only know one four-letter ghost. You know perfectly well who I mean."

"Me!"

I looked up. Anna was descending with a parachute. The closer she came, the more blinding was the white. When Anna landed beside me, I stopped seeing her.

"Close your eyes, Christophe."

I did as she asked. Then I saw her again. It was Anna light.

"Do you want me to eat my bicycle?"

"How old are you, Christophe?"

"I'm seven."

"And you've been seven for how many years now?"

"Ummm ... Are you in pain, Anna?"

"A ghost feels no pain."

"What are you doing inside Fred?"

"This is where four-letter ghosts live. But not for long. Soon we'll have to go elsewhere. Open your eyes!"

I obeyed. She was no longer there. The current grew stronger. Everything exploded. A huge blast of air sent me spinning in every direction. I closed my eyes. That was when I saw Rita. She was surrounded by butterflies of ice. I opened my eyes so I wouldn't see her. But whether they were open or shut, Rita was still visible.

"How old are you, Christophe?"

"What's this obsession with people's ages?"

"Answer me."

"I'm fourteen."

"Now open your eyes."

"They're already open."

"You call that open? Open them!"

I opened them so hard that they fell. I saw them—but with what?—bounce like marbles. I ran after them. Tried to catch up with them. But as soon as I thought that I had, they vanished into the atmosphere. Tired, I let myself drop. But on what? Now everything was fog. A single spot of colour resisted: my heart. Then I spied Fred, standing on his roots. Dancing. No. He wasn't doing anything. It was I who was hopping around him. Fred!

"I am his four-letter ghost. City employees are cutting off my branches."

"No!"

"Don't get excited! You can't expect them to leave me to rot in the middle of Saint-Joseph Boulevard! They're doing their job. You can tell them I'm sorry about the car I squashed. I was trying to avoid a squirrel when I fell. And stop jumping around like that!"

"I don't know why I'm jumping like that."

"You're nervous. How old are you?"

"Not you too!"

"How old are you?"

"Twenty-one."

"Are you sure?"

"No, that's true, I'm twenty-eight. Time flies!"

"It would be best if you go now. The City employees..."

"I can't hear you!"

"Go ... "

"Fred?"

Two men grabbed me by the shoulders. They needed a third man's help to peel me off Fred. The three City employees, wearing yellow uniforms, examined me as if I were crazy. The flasher on a gigantic tow-truck was revolving. The maple had lost all its branches. They were already attacking its trunk with an enormous saw that was screaming into the bark. I tried to throw myself at Fred to protect him. A very fat man in a hard hat immobilized me.

"Mister, how old are you to be acting like that?"

"Thirty-five."

"Let us do our work. Clear out or I call the police. Come on, beat it!"

I made a slight move to leave. Then retraced my steps. I wanted to give Fred one last farewell, but the men in yellow pushed me away without further ado. I left the premises, with a piece of bark in my pockets.

I fell several times. Montreal had been transformed into a skating rink littered with obstacles. The morning sun had warmed the city and it was steaming now. I didn't run into many people. Without car traffic, the streets were starting to look like ice slides. Very quickly the outline of the city became blurred. I thought things over, invisible. Why these four-letter ghosts: Fred, Anna, Rita? And the others I could make out in the fog: life, love, evil? Why was life relentlessly taking me onto slippery roads, towards porous, changing, penetrable beings, so evanescent that they disappeared into the air?

The midday sun partially dispersed the fog. The city reappeared in fragments, in a mise en scène that made it Gothic, surreal, childlike. I found myself in Parc Lafontaine. Rather, on Planet Lafontaine. Nothing seemed to look like what it was. Recumbent trees, piles of overturned roots, split trunks, torn-off branches, and some upright trees, very upright but transfigured by the light, totem poles that dropped precious stones onto the ground. A landscape of scrapes and scratches made painless by beauty. A landscape that didn't stay in place for even a second. That went away, returned, unrecognizable or spuriously lifelike.

A great roar of laughter came over me.

I went back to the apartment to get my Canon. It was hidden under a pile of shoes. I took it out of its case. I hadn't held it in my hands since Mexico. Seven years ago. Time had flown. I went out into the slippery streets again to capture the city's ghost.

ANNALEXICON

In memory of Anna

Annalexicon

ANNA BLAST: abrupt change in the life of someone that leads him or her to experience a crisis of identity, nosebleeds, and no end of trouble come hell or high water. It is rare for anyone to survive two Anna blasts, for if the first leaves you flat as a pancake, the second spins you around like a cabbage roll (controversial dish in Quebec cuisine) in a sauce of bitterness. In Scotland, large-scale bagpipes that need a dozen persons to produce a sound. The clergy had long opposed its use, but with no success. Today, it is valued again and there are several anna blast festivals every spring on Scotland's steep, drenched cliffs. A popular song that lauds its charms and exploits has even travelled round the seven seas. Here is the refrain, which brings back happy memories to more than one listener:

Blow blow
anna blast
drop our masks
swing swing
anna blast
spread our wings

But I, Anna, I have neither the heart to sing nor the lungs to swell. I suffer the anna blast during every second of my existence. I've beaten all endurance records and developed a surprising resistance to the blast of your indifference. If a painter of the symbolic-figurative allegiance wanted to get to the heart of the pangs my soul is suffering, I would suggest that he copy exactly the wriggling of a fish out of water.

ANNA CATASTROPHE: Blonde event that shatters the mirror of the day at the very moment when I plunge into it. Gazing at it opens the eye of the typhoon to the point of blindness. A second that makes time spill over. My time. Reduces the likelihood of my survival. I can't do anything about it, I see you, I drown. I prefer shipwreck—if it's you who causes it—over the grey rescue of sleep.

ANNA DOSE: Unit of measurement used in emergencies. Name given to the small white flowers that grow in foreign countries whose names we always have to look up. Rash that goes with weaning: "To wake up covered with anna dose." Term from pottery that refers to broken jars. Among nomadic desert peoples, a family reunion at which taboos collapse, whence the expression "to sweep up the anna dose" meaning to clean up the mess after a party or, more mundanely, to clean house. In the Caribbean, drink made of layers of different kinds of alcoholic beverages that is offered to the first person who comes along. For Sunday painters, cheap turpentine. For me, it's a reminder of a dream. I was visiting a museum in Mexico. In the Yucatán, probably. I was in a vast, dimly-lit room

with wooden shelves on all four walls. Approaching it, I noticed some small bottles placed here and there, and above each one, an inscription in a language something like Spanish but whose script looked like hieroglyphs midway between drawing and lettering. I came even closer, intrigued, magnetized, filled with sudden expectancy: I was very likely on the verge of a thrilling discovery. But once I practically had my nose in them, I realized that these objets d'art were simply miniature bottles of Coca-Cola. Far from being let down, I was overjoyed. I had just realized all at once—how? I really don't know—that I could decipher the inscriptions. Beneath one, I read: *anna dose, glass, 1988, a critical period known as that of Montreal.* Beneath another: *anna dose, tinted bent glass, 1994, classic period, new formula.* All those bottles were anna doses! I picked one up and thrust it into a ray of light that had just providentially streaked the museum's dim light. I examined it as if it were a diamond and after bedazzlement, I could see inside it a slight movement that had condensed to form a silhouette and an adorable little face: yours. What were you doing, Anna, inside that bottle of Mayan Coca-Cola? You gestured to me with your nose like Jeannie, the bottled genie from *I Dream of Jeannie*. (Later, I realize that even in a dream we get our TV shows mixed up. Actually the sign that Anna sent me was more like the nasal command that accompanied the waving of the magic wand in *Bewitched* than a movement by Jeannie's neck, which I'd mistaken for a movement of the nose, a mistake I'd never have made when I was awake.) I realized that you were asking me to uncap the bottle in which you were imprisoned. Several thoughts bombarded me: 1) I don't have a bottle-opener on me; 2) if I set her free she'll run away and stay away; 3) for once I've got her nearby, I should take advantage of it; 4) how practical—a miniature, portable Anna! 5) poor thing, is that any kind of life, going around and around inside a bottle of Coke? 6) what can Anna have done to deserve such a fate? 7) what with my asthma and allergies, if I were in her place I'd choke to death; 8) look around to see if anyone's watching, then stuff the bottle in your pocket and no one will be the wiser; 9) if I'm caught, it means jail; 10) I don't want to rot and die in a Mexican jail like in the film *Midnight Express* (which is set in Turkey but there you go, I'm confused again); 11) but how to resist Anna's gesture with her nose; 12) yes, how? That was when, brimming over with love for you, I opened the bottle and stuck its neck in my mouth. I broke two front teeth but I forgot about the pain when I heard you laugh. As soon as you'd escaped from the bottle in the form of joyous smoke, you resumed your normal dimensions and galloped away. I tried to grab you, but the museum guard grabbed me by the hair. I had to give him all my American Express travellers' cheques before he let me go, holding the empty bottle. Outside, there was the sea. Green. And the sun. Yellow. I sat down on the blazing sand and then, as I'd done at the museum, I studied the bottle in the daylight. You weren't there any more, but I could see something in the bottom. I shook the bottle and a tiny tuft of blonde hair dropped into my hand. I woke up. In a sweat. As if the Yucatán sun had stayed up all night in my room, just above my bed. Quickly I opened my hand. In my palm was a hair. Just one. I'm not dreaming, I told myself! I switched on the bedside lamp to get a better look. Alas, the hair was black. The whole story about anna dose, the Coke bottle, and the hair troubled me for a long time. I still open my hand every morning to see if I am holding a blonde hair.

ANNA DRAPE: An Australian butterfly, whose male, one-fifth the size of the female, disappears completely between her wings during the annual coitus, and once the act has been accomplished, returns to the state of caterpillar. Disoriented, he inevitably winds up under a tourist's shoe or a koala bear's rough paw, expiating while expiring. The shape of this butterfly inspired a team of Mali engineers and California architects to mass-produce solar panels that took

off at once and sold like hotcakes. These panels are also sensitive to the human warmth released during certain emotional states. New York City foresees that by the year 2010, it will be able to dispense with the services of Hydro-Québec because of the elevated rate of depression in its population, which the anna drapes convert into electricity. But Quebec need not fear for the future. Thanks to the infinite natural resources of my broken heart, all the neon lights of Montreal will shine for a long time yet, enabling it to export heat, light, and sensual pleasure all the way to the Gaspé.

ANNA ECHO: Complex musical form that feeds on its composer's neurons. Some schools of psychiatry define the anna echo as a duplication of the personality. Major critical studies have demonstrated a link between poetry and the anna echo. There are those who maintain that post-modernism is merely a vast wave of anna echo that erases meaning during its successive passages, turning it into non-biodegradable pellets. For historians of the Montreal Côte-des-Neiges neighbourhood school, the anna echo works against the grain, shuffles the cards, and drives everything around in circles. For me, the anna echo is a phone that rings in the deepest part of my heart. To answer it would be fatal. (Anna, I collect all your silences, from *a* to *z*.)

ANNA EMBARGO: In dance, a pas de deux that leads nowhere. The most wonderful anna embargoes astound, glue one to one's seat, give rise to thundering applause—to the amazement of the dancers who, beneath their sweat, are sketching out plans for escape. American TV has got hold of the phenomenon, not without a certain robustness, and imposed it on a target population that is more and more ignorant of its real position in the world. That was how Anna Embargo International (A.E.I.) first saw the light of day, taking advantage of global recession and the satellization of the media to become a must in the salons, hearts, and loins of all nations, whether modern or heading for modernity. The A.E.I. appointed me personally last year, and I had to swallow my TV, cable included, to get back the use of my legs and the power of speech, and to give my eyes a well-earned rest. Eating the impossible, Anna, was the last hope for my limbs that were numb from everything I couldn't do with you, in you, for you.

ANNA ICEBERG: What emerges from the eye after a break-and-enter. A precious alloy found in an airplane's fuselage which, at extreme altitudes, emits a sound that typhoons, hurricanes, and tornadoes pull down to earth, amplifying it with their breath and transforming it by night into vowels. Especially *a*. Used near a streetlamp, it means stroke of genius: "I was hit by an anna iceberg." In temperate lands, a ski trail for those with nothing left to lose. Medical term to designate momentary blindness. Synonym for times are tough, the couldn't-give-a-damn attitude, inner rumbling, waltz, condiment, cranial trauma, etc. Note: In fact, anna iceberg means anything at all, but for one who has tasted the cocaine of your lips, Anna, it denotes ecstasy—virgin, frozen, stupefied all the way to the definitive extinction of colours.

ANNA LETHARGY: Mirror used by the ancient Egyptians during mummification rituals. For a long time it was believed that the function of anna lethargies—always cut out along the facial outline of the person being embalmed—was to prevent the soul from being watered down in space. Many researchers have refuted this thesis, arguing the absence of light from the funeral chambers in the pyramids. Most people, like you and me, are of the opinion that anna lethargy symbolized the vanity of all things: what is a mirror without an image, without a reflection? A film that's on hold, wrapped around itself to the point of suffocation, macerating in the dark like remorse—remorse at not having existed. Perhaps. But I'm sometimes inclined to believe that anna lethargy served quite simply as a rear-view mirror.

ANNA MORTAR SHELL: Internal combustion engine used mainly on hydro-electric mega-projects. The anna mortar shell wipes out everything in its path, scrubs the place, makes the void squeaky-clean, causes people to fall on their backs, on their asses. The side effects of the anna mortar shell aren't covered by Medicare. Expect several lives before you get over it. (Anna, the explosion of your footsteps on the snow one December night haunts me still. That night I understood what kind of person I was dealing with. Why hadn't I been brave enough to tear open the white skin that served as an envelope for the knife of your beauty?)

ANNA PARACHUTE: Another way of saying: "Love gives one wings." By amorous extension, blind and infinite, opening of the chest followed by ejection of the lungs. Common usage: everything white that is produced by love, everything it causes to swell, to get off on, to fall gently back to earth. (Anna, I love you even in parentheses.)

ANNA SKIN: Backdrop used for love stories with unhappy endings. Embroidery popular in eighteenth- and ninteenth-century Rajasthan used in making bedspreads. In Greek mythology, labyrinth where children born without their consent were flung. Later, people enjoyed throwing there whoever and whatever came through the door: frustrated lovers, chipped chamber pots, old magazines, thwarted dreams, broken necklaces. Thus the Greek anna skin is at the origin of the modern dump. When used in the feminine (annagirl skin) all its meanings blink, waver, and vanish into nothingness from where may emerge the only meaning that interests me: the network that your skin offers to my senses and to my sense of direction, which is infinitely shaken up and allows me to go in circles indefinitely.

ANNA SQUAT: Story told to children to expose them to the meaning of death, to its switchback development, to its punctuality. Anna squats exist in every culture and have been the subject of a number of scientific compilations.

Recently, the comic strip and software markets have commandeered the annasquatish contents and turned it into a media circus. Result: children are scared, they run through the streets, they die in gangs. Annasquatism, a recent social phenomenon, has become a wound. It bleeds at dawn, clots at dusk. A significant artistic movement has developed around it. Certain artists have been hit hard and died unknown. (Anna, my photo series, "Whatever Happened to Anna?" is pure annasquatism. Each of those photos cuts reality, splits it open, carves it up according to the luminous stippling of your silhouette and makes possible the elimination of beauty, its arrival in the open air, its promotion to incandescence. You are the flash that gives its light to light. Space, nervous around you, fails to define your parameters. Anna, Anna, you sizzle so in the dust of this world that neither oxide nor anyone can fix you. My poor series falters like a heart.)

ANNA STONY HEART: Character of an impossible thing that's on the verge of no longer being impossible. The pre-Socratic philosophers were the first to define the internal contradictions of the notion of anna stony heart which subsequently (there is always a follow-up to ideas) influenced modern thought; the art of drinking coffee alone while listening to the news on the radio and watching over the dying in large hospitals. The literal sense of anna stony heart was pretty well molten in the twentieth century until it stank, appearing in blotches, in fat deposits. It is used then in moments of stupor, intoxication, and moral impotence. Anna stony heart is also the name given to a carnivorous flower discovered in the Yukon which is believed to be behind the extinction of the mammoths.

ANNA THAT'S ALL: Invisible cul-de-sac that takes everyone by surprise, including me. Name given to hiccups when they go on until each attack is linked to the next, which is also linked to the next and so on until it replaces amazement at being alive with a starchy exclamation rather like a goose being force-fed.

Another name given to *The Tidings Brought to Mary*. In temperate lands, the condition of ski trails in summer, whence the expression "to slip on one's anna that's all," which nowadays is starting to replace "to walk on eggs." (A quick word, Anna: you practise synonymy, *appellation contrôlée*, milky ecstasy, putting one's threat into deadly action, the elongated gaze, the jack-knife dive: you're good at that, too good even, but when will you stop giving off those waves that my panicky sensors swallow, siphon, and pile up, while unable to send back into the open air the love monoxide that is poisoning my existence, my veins, and my breath? I know, I'm ungrateful, I'm a heartbeat away from ignominy, I'm a disgrace to public health, to the march of progress, to the polychrome arrow of postmodern time, I am unworthy of software, of a career plan, and I can only tolerate myself in a state of weightlessness [which is ultra-rare], I know that, know it too well even, but Anna, have you even once paid the pending debts of my boldness, greener than ever?)

ANNA TROU NOIR: French theory of love that rallies all those who are opposed to it. As for me, Anna, I don't give a damn. I believe in your beginning, in your big bang, in your shock wave, in the scratch that time leaves on the eyelids. I knew right away that the black, rectangular slab from the film *2001: A Space Odyssey* was you in the form of compressed anger. Your paint-soaked hair has spattered onto the *t* of totems, the *k* of peaks, the sheet metal of streetcars, and the graffiti that brick and stone have drunk up between their granular rifts. If in Paris one loves, in Montreal one *falls* in love, and that hurts for a long time, it defies understanding, it frees the cortex of its accepted ideas, it lays end to end the twin rails of hatred, it makes bedsheets, the horizon, and horses snap. I studied the theory of anna black hole to the point of anemia, I burned thousands of candle stubs, wore out the seats of my pants, including my pelvic bones, and came late to brandish my brain on the Plexiglas of skyscrapers. I have confused the big hand and the little hand on my watch, the little dipper and the big dipper of my drifting. I have sold my blood to impassive receptacles, I've observed God galloping, taking to his heels, trying to record in his notebook the sketches of your beauty now slipped away. Put into practice, the theory of anna black hole splits me in two, opens my jeans for all eternity, revealing their contents to any travellers of sand and fatigue it encounters. But Anna, what is a hole that sucks up the very edge of the being, turns it over, twists it, and puts it out to pasture in nothingness? What is it, my Anna, if not you and me and this endless blunt refusal? The sky eats, I digest. And I hope for new chapters to your long and astounding theory, even if I can't understand a word.

ANNA WAVE: Loose coat made of canvas or linen very fashionable in post-war France. Worn particularly by poets, existentialists, and those about to commit a robbery or suicide. This coat inspired a whole slew of painters and sculptors rebelling against surrealism, ready to sell their shirt rather than abdicate the predominance of form over substance. The anna wave has thus become the emblem of a movement that has made enough ink flow to sow confusion in people's minds and to disrupt, if not shock, public opinion. The wide sleeves of the coat, its ample cut, prompt concealment and surprise. The anna wave is also the name of a famous musical comedy (*Anna Wa! Anna Wave!*) whose weft is sewn with the white and black threads of love and revolt. The final scene takes place on the Pont-Neuf, from which the young heroine jumps. In the American version, she jumps off the Brooklyn Bridge (which changes everything). She is saved, spectacularly, by the opening of her anna wave; swollen with hope, it transforms her fatal fall into a graceful and refreshing parachute jump, which allows her to land safe and sound on the deck of the ship where her lover, open-armed, receives her like a gift from God. How many times, Anna, with my finger on "pause," (the film version is out on video) have I left you dangling in space?

ANNA ZOO: Cruel geometry that culminates on nights when the moon is full. Among Africans from Mozambique, a fluid given off by the damp earth at dawn, able to take a herd of elephants out of a coma. During the rainy season, dangerous. In the Gaspé, a name given to a frantic dance in which participants trample on shells thrown up by the sea, whence the expression "anna zoo powder." Examples: Throwing anna zoo powder into the wind is pointless. Pouring some into one's wine, ditto. Into one's bath, ditto. (Anna, Anna, your name is a tunnel. Ecstatic, I enter *a*, *entranced* I exit, I swim from *n* to *n* all the way to the end of the darkness. O Cylinder! O Angel! I link your rings until the circle is extinct!)